GW01374636

Girl Who is Hunted

An Ella Porter Mystery Thriller Book 9

Georgia Wagner

Text Copyright © 2024 Georgia Wagner

Publisher: Greenfield Press Ltd

The right of Georgia Wagner to be identified as author of the Work has been asserted in accordance with the Copyright, Designs and Patents Act 1988

All rights reserved.

The book is copyright material and must not be copied, reproduced, transferred, distributed, leased, licensed or publicly performed or used in any way except as specifically permitted in writing by the publishers, as allowed under the terms and conditions under which it was purchased or as strictly permitted by applicable copyright law. Any unauthorised distribution or use of this text may be a direct infringement of the author's and publisher's rights and those responsible may be liable in law accordingly.

'Girl Who is Hunted' is a work of fiction. Names, characters, businesses, organisations, places, events, and incidents either are the product of the author's imagination or are used fictitiously. Any resemblance to actual persons, living or dead, and events or locations is entirely coincidental.

Contents

Chapter 1

The wilderness clawed at Emma's skin, each branch a rake, every stone an accusation. Her feet, raw and numb, betrayed her with every slap against the unforgiving ground, trailing droplets of blood. Puffs of breath fell from her lips, vapor trails in the frigid air, as if her body were shedding pieces of her soul into the Alaskan night.

"Keep . . . moving," the words were a silent mantra timed to every ragged breath. Her pulse pounded in her ears. Cold seeped through the thin silver silk of her blouse and the bare skin of her feet. Her toes were numb, each step clumsier than the last. The sweat that beaded on her forehead quickly froze her loose coppery hair to her scalp.

It hardly mattered. She wouldn't stop. She had faced danger before, she would not give in.

Of course, that had been the danger of urban life, where she understood the rules and made sure she survived, no matter who else paid the cost. And she had succeeded in putting it behind her, making a life as social researcher of off-the-grid living, even though she herself liked a few creature comforts.

But none of that prepared her for this flight alone through the dark wilderness, exposed to the Arctic wind, weaving back and forth across the frozen tundra in a fight for her life.

Above, the helicopter loomed like a beast of prey, its roar closer and closer. Its blades cut swathes in the night sky, scattering the stars with every circle. Its searchlight swept the ground, hunting for her.

She veered stumbling to the left, away from the glare and back into shadow.

"Where are you?" From within the chopper, the question was a whisper torn away by the wind, meant for ears that could not hear it. The eyes of the speaker glistened with anticipation.

Emma couldn't hear the voice, but she felt its intent. Her only thought was escape, sharp as the frozen tundra grass that slashed the soles of her feet. A brief image of the rhinestone heels she'd shed at the start of the chase flickered through her mind, with a stab of surprise that she had ever thought them important. Two days ago, when she'd dressed for a celebratory night on the town, she had had something else in mind. Now, each heartbeat counted down the moments she might have left. The primal part of her brain urged her limbs on, even as the cold turned her feet into frozen slabs of meat.

"Almost there," she promised herself, zigging to the right this time as the helicopter swung round. But where was there? The tundra offered only a few scattered scraggly bushes for shelter.

The mechanical whir of the helicopter screamed like a prehistoric raptor. Fear spiked in her veins. She could feel the downdraft, an icy breath on the back of her neck, claws that tried to push her flat to the ground. She stumbled. She stopped her fall with her hands and used them to push off, like she did in high school track so long ago. She did not notice that her hands, too, now bled. The blood froze on her palms as she ran.

"Can't stop." She willed her legs to move faster despite the spreading numbness. This was a race not just against her pursuers but against the very elements themselves.

Pulse hammering against her temples, Emma risked a glance over her shoulder. There it was—behind and to the left, the black beast of a helicopter smirching the sky, its belly an ominous shadow. The chase had narrowed to breaths and heartbeats.

And then she crested a rise and saw trees on the horizon. Like a thirsty nomad spying an oasis, the sight flooded her with hope. If she could make it to the trees, she could hide. She could make shoes from bark and burrow into pine needles. The landscape was a blur of white and gray as she picked up speed, every tree a specter in the starlight. She urged her clumsy feet on, ignoring the pain. The isolation of Alaska had conspired with her enemies, but in the woods she could hide from her predators like any other vulnerable animal.

She gulped air into her aching lungs. She was so close. Just a few minutes more.

Then, an edge of light illuminated her and the ground around her. She skidded sideways, just as a loud retort split the air. Crack!

A sudden eruption in front of her sent a geyser of dirt, ice and snow skyward. Instinctively, she threw her arms up to shield her face, the sound of the detonation rolling over the tundra like thunder.

A gunshot. A very powerful weapon by the sound of it.

"Damn!" she spat, staggering to regain her footing. Another shockwave blasted the ground beside her. Something hit her arm and chest.

For a moment, her hands flew across her thin shirt and trousers. No blood there. Not a bullet, but debris.

She was still alive. For now.

She thought she heard cawing laughter as the helicopter swooped towards her again, but it must have been her imagination, the rotors drowned out every other sound.

She redoubled her efforts, bare feet slapping against the ruthless ground.

It hurt to breathe, no matter how much air she sucked in. She resented the way her breath condensed, a track in the air for the hunter to follow. Her feet were now mostly numb, relief from the former shooting pain, but her leg muscles burned, hot with the need to survive. Each step forward was defiance.

A few yards more, and she entered the trees. Skeletal, they provided few hiding places. Their branches clawed at her like the fingers of the damned as her feet scrabbled over exposed roots. There *had* to be somewhere to hide, a thicket, the embracing limbs of a conifer, somewhere.

She sagged against a wide trunk, hands on her knees, gasping for breath. That was when she realized that the roar from the helicopter was receding. Her head came up, eyes scraping the horizon behind her. The crescent moon, she saw, had risen, hanging in the sky like a scythe.

Had they given up? She stepped away from the tree to hear and see better.

Another gunshot gave her an answer. Emma flinched as its lethal kiss grazed her earlobe. The sound seemed to ricochet inside her skull. She dropped to a squat.

"Damn!" The curse barely escaped her lips before another shot rang out, embedding itself in the tree trunk, just where her head had been a moment before.

She shoved off like a sprinter again, keeping low and weaving among the trees. Every inhale stabbed her lungs, but she had to keep going. Branches crackled around her, and she wasn't sure whether it was her own passage, the wind, or the hunter that made the noise. Clearly, he had left the chopper to track her on foot and put her in a shroud. She could imagine the crosshairs of his rifle dancing over her figure, his finger poised on the trigger, ready to end her flight.

"Keep moving," she panted, "keep moving, keep moving." It was getting harder and harder to breathe. She felt as though she were drowning, in cold and panic and hopelessness.

Another shot, and a splinter of bark exploded from a trunk ahead. It originated opposite where she expected. She cried out, "God!" the first prayer in her life. How had this happened? She had always been a controller of destinies. Now she was running, a rabbit from a wolf.

"Where are you?" she hissed under her breath, scanning between the trees, across the tundra, for any sign of where the danger lurked. Anger kicked in. She would survive. And she would make them – whoever they were – pay. She had friends—connections. She would call on them to organize retribution.

The helicopter, churning above like a hawk circling prey, interrupted her thoughts and made it impossible to hear the noises on the ground around her. Each bullet that missed was a promise of more to come. Fear clawed up her throat, threatening to unleash a scream into the desolate expanse around her. She choked it back.

It wasn't supposed to be like this. Emma had never imagined her data collection in Alaska would morph into a macabre survival game. But here she was, hunted like vermin.

A bullet seared the space where she had been a heartbeat earlier. Emma ducked and swerved, gasping. She knew she couldn't outrun bullets, but she could make herself a harder target. Keep moving. Never straight. Unpredictable as the Arctic winds.

The trees ended in a clearing, several hundred feet wide, with fallen trunks crisscrossing it like crazy fencing.

The chopper's spotlight slashed a path across the clearing.

No. Too dangerous. She backed in among the trees. "Just a little longer . . ." she murmured. Another shot. She dived sideways. The bullet pinged off the frozen ground to her left, sending a shower of ice crystals into the air. They glittered momentarily in the helicopter's light before falling back to earth and disappearing into the snow.

She understood now that she was like those crystals, easily blasted, quickly forgotten. It wasn't just the relentless drone from above; the sniper always seemed to know where she would go next. A ghost with a gun, he was cloaked in the land itself, exacting his own vengeance in this white hell.

Once again, the helicopter veered away. Another noise reached her ears – a faint echo of mirth, guttural and gleeful. Almost instantly, a moan of wind overcame it.

Laughter? No, it couldn't be. But it teased the edges of her hearing, discordant against the lonely wind. It was the sound of madness. Her own, or someone else's? She didn't have time to consider the origin; her survival hinged on movement.

She lurched into the clearing, her feet fully numb now, reeling like a drunk between the stumps and logs. And then lights flooded the space again, this time pulsing from the ground to her right: headlights of a Jeep. The beacons were like a lighthouse in the storm of her plight. Could it be? Respite? Rescue?

"Help," she panted. The wind whisked the word. But she focused on the flashing lights, whose rhythm matched the pounding of her heart. They beckoned, promising safety—or betrayal. There was no telling which until she was close enough to distinguish friend from foe.

She staggered closer, each step jarring her bones. The lights grew stronger, but so did the pain radiating up her legs, the ache in her lungs, the chill biting her skin. She blinked against the light, raising her hand to shield her gaze. She did not notice that the tips of her fingers had begun to darken. All she could really see was the sleek black of the Jeep's grill and hood. She realized in surprise that the gunshots had ceased. Was the sniper out of ammo? Or just reloading?

She nearly tumbled forward to close the gap between her and the Jeep. "Please," she whimpered, even before she could see the driver. The plea was a gamble, a throw of the dice with her life in the balance.

Then she heard that eerie laugh again, behind her. She whirled but saw no one. The laughter hovered in the breeze.

The Jeep's engine growled with power and menace. Coming alongside, she could see a man in the driver's seat, his fingers tapping out a jaunty rhythm on the steering wheel. He wore black leather biker's pants and a drab parka. Its bear-fur hood framed his face and blended with his dark beard. His free hand toyed with a knife, the blade catching the staccato flash from the emergency lights. He smiled at her, a man enjoying a show.

"You!" Not a friend, definitely not a friend. She stepped back, alarmed.

"Yes, me," he agreed, conversationally. "Out here all alone? You're not really dressed for it." His eyes crinkled in amusement.

She threw her last dice. "Help me." She realized with shame that her voice shook. "Please?"

“Help you? My dear, I arranged this for you. Thought it might teach you a lesson.” He swung his legs out of the Jeep. She stumbled back. Seeing it, his smile widened into the grin of a tiger about to pounce.

He hefted the knife, sauntered toward her.

Emma's response was a breathless push to the left, veering away from the rutted track of the Jeep towards the further grove of trees. Her muscles coiled and uncoiled in a rhythm born of desperation. She hadn’t seen a gun in the car. But the knife – she could almost feel it at her throat.

"Running will get you nowhere!" the man taunted from behind. Emma let the words fall away into the night, discarded and irrelevant. Running was her only chance. But, oh, she was so tired. Suddenly she understood how predators could run their prey to exhaustion.

She burst into the woods. The grove was thin, maybe 50 feet across, but the trees were spruce, their thick branches sweeping the ground. Hiding places? Then, between the trunks ahead, she saw a glinting ribbon of ice. A river or a stream?

Jerking forward, she discerned it was indeed a small river. On the other side were more conifers, and a shadow that might be a building. Thoughts fragmented, like the ice she envisioned beneath her feet — stay alive, keep moving, survive. She came out of the trees at the edge of the bank.

The river spread before her, its frozen surface uneven and pierced with fallen branches. Now she could see that not one but two low buildings huddled among the stand of conifers across the river. Moonlight glinted on windowpanes which otherwise remained dark. A farm? People and safety? The faint hope drove her on.

She skidded onto the ice, her bare feet slipping like those of a frightened fawn. She flapped her arms for balance, sliding and stumbling towards the far bank. Her breaths came in short, sharp gasps that did little to satisfy her screaming lungs.

She forced herself to look only ahead. Emma's focus narrowed to the simple mechanics of motion — push, glide, balance, repeat, the jerks of an automaton.

A flock of birds rose up from the trees ahead, smudges against the star-studded sky.

Why? Was the chopper coming back?

No, no, it was that rasping laugh. Another laugh joined in– unstoppable, mocking hilarity, echoing across the ice.

Emma could not feel her feet at all now. She felt her life force ebbing, the drumbeat of her pulse in her ears slowing. Despite her flailing efforts, the opposite shore seemed no closer. She glanced over her shoulder just as the taunting pealed out again. The man with the knife stood on the bank, head thrown back in unholy joy. He made no move to follow her.

"Can't outrun Death, sweetheart!" he called out, almost affectionately. He had hardly finished speaking when a crack of gunfire blasted from the left.

A hot lash seared Emma's upper arm, and she slithered sideways, nearly losing her footing on the slick surface. Blood welled up from the graze, freezing and gluing the silk of her shirt against her skin. Pain radiated from elbow to shoulder, but fear propelled her forward, each step in defiance of fate.

Mockery chased her, howling with the wind. No, it wasn't the wind that howled, it was the chopper returning to the hunt.

The ice stretched before her. She had interpreted it as a path to freedom. Now she imagined the pull of the water beneath the frozen crust, an abyss waiting to claim her. Maybe that would be the real freedom: to fall through, to choose to sleep forever, to deny those predators their trophy.

Suddenly, another gunshot.

The ice below her feet cracked. Before she could hobble further, the surface seemed to shudder, then let go a sigh. A gaping maw opened beneath her. There was no time to scream. Water, merciless and frigid and ravenous, swallowed her whole. Immediately, she knew that this was not better. It, too, was defeat.

She fought, thrashing, as the cold burned every inch of skin. Her lungs contracted, rejecting the water. Her head and hands, fueled by impotent rage, pounded against the ice above her, beating it as she wanted to beat the men hunting her.

A sudden light from above bounced off the crust overhead, except for one spot ahead where it permeated the water, shimmering into the deep. She kicked in that direction. Somehow her fingertips found the hole in the ice. Somehow, they guided her head above water. Somehow, she sucked in new blessed air and waited for the roaring in her ears to subside.

But the roaring was the chopper. She blinked repeatedly to open wide her frozen eyelids, then squinted as the spotlight from above blinded her. The helicopter shifted position, and suddenly she could see what hunted her.

It wasn't a man.

A gray beast crouched on the ice staring at her. It had dead dark eyes. Its mouth was a gashed rictus.

It was larger than any wolf she'd ever seen, almost as broad as a bear. As her mind struggled to make sense of what she saw, the creature bared its teeth and lunged forward.

Pain pierced her throat.

She saw nothing as the blood dyed the water around her and spread out under the ice. She felt nothing as the current pulled her down a second time. But the last thing she heard was the growling mirth of the beast.

Chapter 2

It was morning, but not a good morning. Ella Porter sat rigid beside Brenner Gunn in a helicopter cockpit, her gaze affixed to the bleak landscape below as the aircraft approached Nome. Miles and miles of nothing, the snowy tundra only occasionally punctuated by signs of life: a cluster of thickets, a grazing herd of caribou.

They were returning from a debriefing in the capital, Ella's with the FBI, Gunn's with the U.S. Marshal's Office. Usually such things were routine, marking an end to a case.

But today the case had involved the death of Ella's father. And there was nothing routine about that. Her own soul felt like the landscape below, but without a sign of life.

As they flew, a few roads cut the wilderness, radiating out from Nome. Soon the chopper reached the outskirts of the city, a patchwork of a few hundred houses hugging the coast and fanning towards the wilderness. From her vantage point Ella could see the homes' bright colors, defiantly cheerful against the glowering grays of sea, sky, and tundra. Usually the incongruously tropical reds, blues, greens, and purples made Ella smile. Today, however, the gaiety seemed forced and futile.

The radio crackled, and Ella frowned as the pilot spoke through her headphones. "Trouble waiting on the tarmac below. We need to prep."

"What sort of trouble?" Ella's voice sounded brusquer than she intended.

"Some sort of demonstration. Not sure what. Waiting to hear."

Ella glanced out the window, peering through the glass, but it was impossible to see much through a sky streaked with falling snow.

"Looks like we're in for some weather," Brenner remarked, his voice barely audible over the thrumming blades.

"Seems fitting," Ella murmured. Both her companions had sat up straighter. She could feel the unease permeating the air in the cabin, an electric charge from the storm around them as well as the conflict that seemingly awaited on the ground.

Ella pulled her jacket tighter around her as if the chill from the snow had seeped into the cabin. She was a small woman, and the motion briefly shrank her further into herself. The dark blue of her puffy parka contrasted with the pallor of her skin. Her blond hair was drawn back into a severe ponytail that emphasized new hollows in her cheeks and under her deep-set blue eyes. Her tip-tilted nose contrasted with the severe set of her lips. To the pilot, casting a glance backwards, she looked both beautiful and unapproachable, an ice princess.

Brenner Gunn, by contrast, shifted to see around her headset, his eyes a sea of concern. "You holding up okay?" His words breathed empathy, incongruous with his rugged exterior. He was tall, over six feet. Even sitting, he towered over Ella. He had dark hair cut short that curled slightly across his forehead, even features, a defined jaw and high cheekbones. A pale burn scar, a souvenir of his time as a SEAL in Iraq, puckered his left cheek, running from chin to ear. Without the scar, he might have qualified as a male model for some luxury watch brand. As it was, he was her closest friend.

Ella gave a slight nod but remained silent. Words felt like unnecessary noise against the roar of her internal turmoil--was it grief? Anger?

Both...

Her father, taken from her by the elusive figure known only as the Architect. A hurricane of sorrow and regret churned inside her...

"Listen, Ella," Brenner leaned toward her, his broad shoulders inside his gray U.S. Marshal jacket shielding her somewhat from the pilot's curious gaze. "Whatever happened with your old man... it's not on you. You did everything you could."

"Did I?" Doubt flattened her voice. "I keep replaying it all, wondering if there was a moment, a single decision that could've changed everything."

"Hey," Brenner put his hand on her near shoulder. He had massive paws, used to handling a sniper's rifle and miscreants. "You can't think like that. It'll eat you alive. You did everything you humanly could." His touch was a comfort and a reminder.

Ella turned to meet his gaze, finding an anchor in the shared pain reflected there. Brenner, too, had lost someone to the chaos of their lives—his child with Priscilla. Yet here he was, still steady alongside her.

The helicopter began its descent, the landing pad coming into view amidst the swirling eddies of snow.

Ella shook her head as they descended, clearing the cobweb of emotions from the forefront of her mind. She knew Brenner was right. She could not afford to let brooding corrode her thoughts, not with other tasks to deal with right now. She leaned forward in her seat and touched her earpiece as she addressed the pilot. "Any word on what that trouble is?"

The pilot said, "Er... yeah. Your sister."

"Priscilla? What about her?"

"She's... causing a scene. She's got a crowd there to help her."

Suddenly, the helicopter swung and jolted as they touched down, but it was nothing compared to the sinking sensation in Ella's stomach. All her sickening thoughts returned in a rush.

Her sister... Priscilla...

There was no world in which Cilla was going to understand. Cilla had demanded Ella keep their father safe.

Now what was Ella supposed to say? To do?

She opened the door of the helicopter as the whirring blades above them began to slow. Cold slapped at her cheeks, but she knew her sister would hit harder and deeper. She exited the copter with a dancer's easy grace. Brenner followed, unfolding himself stiffly and rubbing his bad hip.

Ella's boots crunched the gravel of the landing pad as she headed toward the terminal. Her breath hung in the chill as Brenner fell into step beside her. The airport was a hive of commotion, in contrast to the desolate terrain just outside the city. The swirling snow muffled but could not hide the shuffle of feet and conversations. As Ella and Brenner rounded the terminal – really, a glorified warehouse plunked down in the middle of the tarmac – a shrill voice pierced the snowfall.

Priscilla stood on the hood of a bright yellow pickup truck emblazoned with the words, "Porter Mining." The sea-shell earrings she wore glinted like ivory-handled daggers as she raged before a group of burly men clad in denim and yellow and black parkas--miners from her company no doubt. A handful of police and airport security officers stood watch.

Priscilla's neat figure was clad in silver cashmere trousers and a puffy black jacket lined with grey fox fur, its hood down. Her pretty face – the mirror of Ella's – contorted in anger, and the blonde hair wild about her face gave her the look of Medusa. Her gloved hands swiped impatiently at the snow that caught in her eyelashes, but her tirade never stopped. "It's a conspiracy! A cover up! And we won't let them get away with it!"

The crowd, muttering along, burst into shouts. "No! No, we won't!"

Ella had been expecting trouble, but not something so... direct. Then again, given her sister's personality, she should've known.

"Pris," Ella murmured under her breath, her heart aching for her sister. She slowed her stride, easing up to the fray.

"Keep walking, El," Brenner instructed, his hand at her elbow. Yet as he shifted them towards the parking lot, his eyes remained fixed on the unfolding spectacle, evaluating danger. "She's just looking for an audience."

Ella knew he was right, but she couldn't tear her gaze away from her twin. Where Ella felt doubt and regret, Priscilla channeled grief into hatred. Priscilla jumped down from her makeshift podium and landed on the snowy tarmac like a gymnast. She pointed an accusatory finger at the semi-circle of officers who stood with arms crossed and clubs in their hands.

"You!" Priscilla's voice cracked like a whip. "You're all in on this cover-up. My father deserved better!"

"Ma'am, please step back." One officer stepped forward, his club raised, his free hand resting near his holster. "This is not the place—"

"Like hell it isn't!" A miner surged forward, his face flushed with solidarity, and shoved the officer. The latter fell backwards onto the tarmac. His club bounced sideways, and the miner grabbed it up.

Pandemonium erupted as more miners rushed in, their frustration erupting into physical release. The officer in charge was yelling, "Hold your fire" even as miners tackled the squad. Police returned blows with fists and billy clubs, but they lacked shields and were far outnumbered. The fight became a brawl, the miners heaving with rage. Priscilla had scrambled back into the bed of the pickup, where she stood watching, a goddess of wrath.

"Damn it," Brenner cursed, grabbing Ella closer and pulling her to the side, out of the direct path of the melee. "We don't need to get caught up in this mess too."

"Let me go, Brenner!" Ella tried to shake off his grasp, torn between duty and the boiling blood of kinship. "I have to stop her before she gets hurt."

"Look at me, El!" Brenner swung himself between her and the brawl, forcing her to pay attention. "Your sister is past listening, and you're no good to anyone if you get dragged into that pit."

The words stung, but truth often did. Ella winced but held back as she watched an officer with a bleeding nose tackle a miner to the ground. Handcuffs glinted in the waning winter light. Priscilla was screaming now, her voice hoarse as she incited her followers.

"Come on," Brenner urged, tugging at her again. "Before some-one gets seriously hurt."

Ella allowed him to pull her back, each step away from the fray feeling like a betrayal. But beneath the layers of sorrow and regret, she knew Brenner was right. This was Priscilla's battle; one she had chosen for herself.

And then Priscilla's eyes, roving over her battlefield, saw Ella.

Cilla's blue eyes bulged. A different, deeper fury twisted her snow-streaked features. Her fists balled at her sides. "You!" Cilla screamed. "You're the one we're here for! You--you bitch!" Her voice shook the sky. On the ground, the scuffle between the miners and the cops paused.

Ella didn't notice anyone except for her twin sister. For a moment, blue eyes stared into blue.

Then Cilla vaulted over the pickup's tailgate, and without stopping, stalked towards her sister. The miners parted silently, men craning their heads to see this new source of drama. Cilla bared her teeth. "You killed him!" she screamed. "You promised to keep him safe! You promised!"

Ella said nothing. What could she say? It was true. She had promised, and she had failed in her promise. She stood still, waiting. Each scream from Cilla was like a knife slicing into Ella's soul. So this is what justice feels like, she thought.

"Ella, come *on*. Let's go. No point." Brenner's voice cut across her consciousness. She looked away from Cilla's mad fury into his insistent and steady blue gaze. Something there reminded her to breathe.

“OK,” she said.

As they retreated, the sound of sirens swelled in the distance, converging on the scene. Ella glanced over her shoulder one last time to see Priscilla being restrained by two officers. Cilla's wild eyes met Ella's for a fleeting moment, full of fire and accusation.

"Let's get out of here," Brenner's voice dragged her attention away from her sister again. "Car's waiting for us up ahead."

The airport's concrete was a cold, indifferent gray, mirroring the skies above. Brenner's firm grip on her arm felt like the only thing tethering Ella to the world as they navigated through the sea of parked vehicles. His limp was barely noticeable, but she knew every step demonstrated his resilience in the face of suffering—a trait she desperately needed now.

"Watch your step," Brenner cautioned, guiding Ella around a slick of ice that reflected the churning gray clouds. They reached a nondescript black sedan, its ordinariness a contrast to the chaos they left behind.

"Get in," he said, opening the front passenger door with an efficiency that spoke of his military past.

Ella hesitated, the image of Priscilla's enraged face flashing in her mind. Then, with a deep breath, she slid into the car's sanctuary, feeling the faux leather embrace her like a protective shell. As Brenner closed the door, the sounds of the airport faded into a distant hum.

The vibration of her phone destroyed the moment of calm. The screen displayed "Agent Johnson", her superior in Seattle. What could he want?

"Porter," she answered calmly, professionalism overcoming the emotions of the last few minutes, as Brenner slipped into the driver-side seat.

"Porter, this is Johnson." His voice was crisp and formal, far more formal than the officer who had interviewed her during the morning debriefing. Johnson's tone was a harbinger of bad news, she could tell. "We've had a formal complaint lodged against you questioning your competence and probity. It's serious."

Ella's skin prickled. She gripped the phone tighter. She could almost feel the weight of her badge, heavy in her pocket.

"Formal complaint?" Her measured words concealed the sudden tightness in her chest.

"Yes, it's being processed as we speak," Johnson continued.

"Who filed it?"

"The sheriff in Nome."

The sheriff in Nome. Priscilla's husband. Doing his wife's dirty work, no doubt. And yet, Cilla's mob had just assaulted the police. Was Cilla losing it?

Ella wondered if she should have expected this. The sound of paper shuffling on the other end seemed to underline the thought. Definitely, she should have expected something. "So ... what does this mean?" she asked Johnson. She kept her voice even, but it took all her self-control. She could feel Brenner's gaze on her. She turned away to hide her face.

Ella had been assigned to the single-agent field office in Nome after a stellar rise in Seattle. The "assignment" was disciplinary demotion after she'd allowed a serial killer to escape custody. After several years, Nome had become something of a home. Now, she could hear the tightness in the Seattle SA's voice.

"What was the complaint, sir?"

"I'm not at liberty to say yet. But given the circumstances, the decision has been made to loan you out, away from the FBI."

Ella's heart sank. "Loan?"

"Just for a little bit, while we smooth things over."

Emma allowed this information to digest before speaking again. "Who am I being loaned to, sir?"

"To the Marshals. They need an experienced agent as liaison. We figured with Marshal Gunn's assist, you'd be able to repay the favor." He paused. "You might be sent into the backcountry. Or maybe Juneau. Depends which way the case goes."

"You're sending me to Juneau," Ella repeated. "When? And what's the case?" She was not going to let Johnson know how much this had caught her off-balance. Was this the FBI's way of sidelining her? And yet, Juneau was the state capital. Was this a back-handed move up?

"Let's just see what you make of it, Porter," Johnson said, evading her questions. "Be ready to move." The line went dead.

She sat there, blinking, as if she'd just been slapped. Already today, she'd been debriefed for hours concerning the death of her father before being packed onto that chopper and sent home. She'd thought she was in the clear... But now, it felt like walls were closing in.

She faced Brenner again. "Johnson says I'm being loaned out," Ella murmured, more to herself than to Brenner.

Brenner's eyes met hers, his expression unreadable. He started the car and pulled away smoothly, as if the world outside hadn't just shifted beneath her feet.

She leaned back, closing her eyes as she tried to process the implications. What game was Priscilla playing now, using her husband's influence like this?

"Loaned where?"

"To you guys."

"Marshals?"

"Like I said." She glanced at him, wrinkling her nose. "He says there is a case... you heard anything about it?"

"A new one? No. I haven't been told anything."

"Huh. That normal?"

"Usually I don't know until it's across my desk."

"Right..." She chewed on her lower lip, mind flitting from trouble to trouble and back again.

Brenner executed a smooth turn toward downtown. "How come we Marshals are so lucky?"

"What?"

"Why the reassignment?"

"Cilla and her husband have filed a complaint against me with the regional office. Johnson said he's reassigning me until hot feelings cool down. I'm not sure I believe him."

"Has he lied to you before?"

"Nooo, but I know he thinks I'm a pain in his neck."

"Well, you are," Brenner chuckled, a rare sound. Ella returned a wry smile. "But it's part of your charm. Besides, you're too good to let go. Johnson knows that. Whatever it is Cilla and Co. have cooked up, you'll handle it," Brenner said confidently, focusing on the road ahead. "You always do. And a new case will give you something else to focus on while you figure this out."

Ella nodded. She would welcome a new case. Part of her needed it, grasping at anything where she could use her skills. Keeping busy, she could immerse her mind into a problem outside of her own. Something to solve. Something to prove her competence, at least to herself.

But another part of her wanted a new case simply to pull her away from the abyss of her warring emotions and to help her escape unscathed.

Ella felt the car accelerate. She shifted in her seat, frowning out the window at the snowflakes whirling in front of the windshield, sweeping in waves across the gray asphalt, and beating against the doors of the houses and shops on the side of the street.

Brenner eased off on the accelerator and, with a flick of his finger, increased the speed of the windshield wipers. They flung the snow back and forth, a visible metaphor for the emotions in her chest.

Brenner's phone rang from its dashboard stand. He frowned, declining the call while still navigating the vehicle. A minute later, it rang again.

This time, he pulled to the side of the road in front of a hardware store with red shovels displayed in the front window. He picked up the phone. "Gunn," he said. "Yes, sir. She's here. Yes. I heard."

Ella pushed back a stray blonde tress to watch him closely. A quizzical frown furrowed his brow. "When? Right now? Oka y... yeah, we can do that."

She stared at his profile as he hung up. "Boss?"

"Yeah," he said, still frowning as he pulled the car back into traffic. "Wants the deputy Marshals in. Like... right now."

"Now?" It was almost evening, and the day was winding down. But Brenner pushed the speed on his vehicle, hanging a left to turn the hood towards the Marshal Office. "Sounded urgent," he muttered. "He told me to bring you."

Ella crossed her arms, staring out at the snow. A case always entailed learning about someone else's pain, resolving some of the fallout from someone else's tragedy. And yet, she recognized that her larger immediate emotion had nothing to do with empathy. What she felt was relief. Focusing on someone else's trouble meant she could take her eyes off of her own.

A little ashamed of her anticipation, she kept her eyes on the road as Brenner navigated them through the flurry.

Chapter 3

The fluorescent lights of the U.S. Marshal's briefing room flickered, casting a sterile glow over the assembly of faces, all of them male but her own. Ella shifted in the brown folding chair, her gaze fixed on the map of Alaska sprawling across the front wall—a web of white expansiveness with red pins marking the hunting grounds of their quarry.

"Alright, people," Chief Deputy Callum Whiler's voice boomed in the small room. "I don't need to tell you how critical this operation is." He was a bear of a man, in a gray long-sleeved waffle-knit tee that hugged his broad shoulders and sturdy arms, green camouflage pants, and high-ankled boots. His black vest, gray hat and utility belt lay on the table before him, pushed off to the side to make room for a pile of papers. "We've got an escalation in illegal hunting tourism. It's our job to put a stop to it before it gets any worse."

Ella scanned the room, the faces of Brenner's colleagues mirrored the gravity of the situation as well as puzzlement. Marshals did not usually track poachers. It wasn't unheard of, but it wasn't common either. Brenner adjusted his position, his leg brushing against hers, a silent pillar of support. The room had ten occupants, many of the deputy marshals having been brought in from larger Alaskan cities to aid in the operation.

"Nome has been bleeding wildlife," Whiler continued, his finger jabbing at the blood-red pins. "Tourists are paying big money for the thrill of the hunt—money that buys silence and compliance. But not ours." His eyes swept the room, locking onto each agent in turn.

"Tell us about the perp," someone called from the back.

"Name's Miles Cruise," Whiler answered, flipping to a slide showing a grainy photo of a rugged man clad in biker leathers. His smile did little to mask the coldness in his eyes. He had an enormous brown beard that gave him the look of a lumber jack. "Ex-marine, ex-con turned poacher. Uses his connections to lure thrill-seekers into illegal hunts. He thinks he's untouchable."

Ella studied the face of Miles Cruise. He had a haughty tilt to his chin, and his eyes stared coldly into the camera.

"Miles operates predominantly at night," Whiler said. "His clients want the full experience—the danger, the adrenaline. He gives it to them, for a price. And they cheat – firing from helicopters and Jeeps, using lights to flush out game. Mostly they take heads for trophies and leave the carcasses to rot. Except for walruses – they're killing them for the tusks."

Brenner jotted notes down, his brow furrowed. Ella observed him for a moment, wondering what went through his mind as he scribbled.

"Our mission is clear," Whiler's voice brought her back. "Track him down, dismantle the operation, and bring him to justice."

Ella's thoughts raced. She felt something of a relief to be distracted from the direction her thoughts wanted to go. Priscilla, her father... it could all be pushed aside for now. She had other things to worry about.

"Questions?" Whiler barked, breaking Ella's reverie.

Brenner raised a hand. “How come we’re involved? Isn’t this something that Fish and Wildlife usually handle?”

A couple other marshals murmured assent.

“Good question,” approved Whiler. “We’re taking it out of their hands because we’ve been given some intel.”

“What intel?” the man in front of Ella prodded.

“That Cruise’s gang is covering up at least one human death.”

This caused a collective buzz of interest. Ella leaned forward.

“One of the hunters?” asked the guy in the front row. “Like, a hunting accident?”

"It could be one of the hunters," Whiler said. "But our intel says it was no accident."

It seemed like everyone in the room stopped breathing for a moment. Ella's hands closed over the edge of her seat. If the intel was true, then Johnson's reassignment was not just a sideline. This was an important case.

"Who told us? One of the clients?"

Whiler lifted both palms in a shrug. "Anonymous tip. But other aspects of the story check out, so we are taking it seriously."

"Where do we start?" someone from the back row asked.

"Intel suggests that Cruise finds most of his clientele at local bars," Whiler replied. "Rumor has it Scott and Clean is where he's been recruiting."

A bar. Ella's spirits lifted ever so slightly. Bars meant people, conversations, leads. They could work with that.

Whiler faced the group again and he pointed at Ella. "Our federal friends have been kind enough to provide a liaison. They've had run-ins with Miles Cruise in the past, and so the agency has assured me their full resources are at our disposal."

Ella was nonplussed. It wasn't usually like the feds to get involved in a poaching case, even one with rumors of homicide. What did Whiler mean, they'd had run-ins with the poacher?

She glanced at him, but he didn't quite hold her gaze.

Something felt off, gnawing at her, but then Whiler started to speak again.

"Mayor Hancock is all over my ass about this," Whiler's mouth turned down. "He wants Cruise in cuffs before the next news cycle. Media vultures are circling, ready to feast on whatever story comes out of this mess."

"Then let's not disappoint them," Brenner called out. "Give 'em a good one."

A couple of his colleagues shouted agreement.

Whiler's voice silenced the cheers. "The stakes couldn't be higher," he declared. He began to pace back and forth in front of the table, his looming shadow on the screen behind punctuating every move.

Ella felt the weight of those words settle over her like the blanket of fresh snow outside the briefing room window. She glanced at Brenner, his profile as resolute as an Alaskan mountain, his attention fixed on Whiler.

"Cruise is no amateur," Whiler continued, clicking to the next slide. "Evidence exists from Interpol that he's done some dirty work in Europe. He's evaded capture before; knows how to cover his tracks. Now, it seems, he's come to Alaska." A map flickered into view, red dots scattered like drops of blood across the image. "These are his last known hunting sites."

Brenner cocked his head, brow furrowed. "Nighttime hunts," he murmured, meditatively. "Means we're looking for someone who doesn't mind the cold... or the dark."

"Exactly." Ella tilted her blonde head towards his dark one. "He hunts like a bobcat, or a wolf, stalking at night when his prey settles down to sleep, letting down their guard."

"Remember, Cruise is more than a poacher," Whiler continued, locking eyes with Ella. "He may be a killer. Now, I've paired you all off. Gunn, you're taking our liaison. Jameson, you're with O'Connor." He continued, running down the list and pointing out the other Marshals.

As he did, Brenner nudged Ella's shoulder with his own. "Who's this Cruise guy?"

"No idea. Not sure why the FBI is involved."

He gave her a long look.

She found herself frowning, wondering exactly what she'd been thrown into.

Chapter 4

They paused outside the entrance to the *Scott and Clean* bar, the muffled sounds of laughter and clinking glasses seeping through the cheap brown siding. Ella met Brenner's eyes, an unspoken signal passing between them. They were about to step into a possible lion's den, but they were hunters too.

Nome was a place for those who lived rough. The weather was rough, the trades were rough, and the Bering Sea was rough. Scott and Clean fit the theme, a large, wooden structure that looked like a cross between a small warehouse and a large bait shop, its paint peeling and weather-beaten. A ratty bamboo blind covered the picture window, hiding the inside from curious outsiders. The only thing that marked it out as a bar was the flickering neon sign hanging above the door that read, "*Scott and Clean—The Last Drop.*"

Brenner and Ella stepped inside, the smell of stale beer hitting them like a punch in the face. The air was thick with smoke and the sound of laughter. Tacky, neon-lit signs advertising cheap drinks and wild times adorned the chipped plaster walls, as did a few unrepaired holes the size of a man's fist.

"Remember, eyes open, blend in," Brenner advised as he shut the door behind them, the warm air clashing with the cold.

"Mhmm," Ella replied, stepping into the din of the bar. She refrained from pointing out that Brenner's height and good looks would mark him out in almost any company. Her own gloves and jacket helped conceal her features and form from prying eyes. She was just a gal out for a drink with some guy.

The Scott and Clean bar throbbed with the forced gaiety of Nome's night owls, a cacophony of clashing conversations and laughter. The musky scent of sweat joined those of spilled beer and hazy tobacco—a perfect cover for the stench of guilt that Ella was certain permeated the room. Though perhaps that scent was one she'd brought with her.

She leaned against the bar, scrutinizing the patrons.

At a table laden with empty bottles and half-eaten plates of food, a boisterous group threw their heads back in laughter, their guffaws ringing out like alarm bells. Ella's gaze lingered on them, searching for any hint of recognition, any slip of conversation that might betray a link to Cruise and his operation.

"See the guy over there, nursing his whiskey?" Brenner had joined her at the bar. He nodded toward a solitary figure at the opposite end of the bar, his eyes obscured by the brim of a weathered baseball cap. "Looks like he's waiting for something ... or someone."

Ella's fingers curled around a frost-kissed glass that had been abandoned half-drunk on the bar's sleek surface. She lifted it and idly swirled the amber liquid within, a prop for her role as well as something to hold on to. The ice within clinked like a warning. The neon lights droned overhead, casting a lurid glow that painted everyone in garish shades of complicity.

She watched the man in the corner, but his head slumped after a bit, and a few seconds later, it sounded as if he were snoring on the bar.

"How good is the intel?" she murmured under her breath.

"Whiler wouldn't give it if it wasn't good," Brenner said quietly. He almost sounded defensive, but she didn't call it out.

Brenner kept his eyes focused on a far corner, his peripheral vision taking in the rest of the bar as he listened to the chatter around them. "So Miles Cruise, eh? What do we know about him?"

Ella sighed, tapping her fingertips against the wet bar, her mind weaving through the threads of information they had on this man. "Not much. Like I told you, even on my end I haven't heard the name."

"So you know what I know?"

"Yeah. Just that he's a poacher and has evaded capture before. I didn't know the feds cared about this sort of thing."

Brenner nodded, looking around as if trying to locate a friend. "That's what I was thinking."

Ella rattled her drink again. "I checked my email to see if any files had come through, but no luck. So I called the Seattle HQ. Johnson was out, but the night officer said he'd left a message for me."

"What message?" Brenner cocked his head.

"*Use your initiative*," Ella quoted. "Whatever that means. Tonight I'm flying blind." She shrugged.

The man at the end of the bar was slumbering now, his snores reverberating in the raucous place. Ella turned to watch a few men playing darts.

The three men at the dartboard seemed to be in their own world, a camaraderie bound by the thwacks of the darts hitting the cork. As one got ready to throw, face set in concentration, the others stepped back, pint glasses in hand, watching as the thrower's shoulder tensed as he drew back his forearm and let the projectile fly. As soon as the dart hit the board the others raised their glasses and laughed, joshing the skill or lack thereof of the thrower. Each missile left a scar on the target, a glistening residue built up over the years.

Ella smiled at their enjoyment. It had been a while since she had had similar light-hearted fun. But something else caught her eye... a figure standing near the dart players.

The man behind was a shadow, his face obscured by the brim of his brown baseball cap and the hood of his dun-colored anorak. He seemed to blend into the wood of the walls. Only his hands moved, flexing and unflexing, betraying anxiety. No, Ella amended, not anxiety. Excitement. Painful, almost unbearable excitement.

He shifted side to side, his breath coming in quick pants. As he shifted, she spotted a weapon on his hip. It wasn't uncommon for the denizens of Nome to carry. In fact, this late at night, she would've been surprised if they hadn't. But there was something about the weapon he had on him. A sidearm she thought she recognized.

She nudged Brenner, and keeping her voice low, said, "What do you think of Mr. Hoodie's coat peashooter?"

Brenner glanced over, surveyed quickly. "Hunter's gun," he said after a moment. "Revolver. Won't jam."

"If, let's say, an angry bear is charging you?"

"Exactly. Iron sight. Good for a charging animal."

Brenner rattled this off as if they were throwaway observations, continuing to survey the hunter from under half-closed lids.

As they watched, anorak man checked his watch, then turned sideways and rapped on a door in the wall. A second later, the door opened. The man in the coat and cap was ushered through by someone out of sight, then the door closed again.

Ella and Brenner put down their fake drinks in unison and began meandering towards that door. Brenner led the way, weaving through the maze of bodies and tables, clasping Ella's hand lightly as if she were his date. Ella smiled vapidly as she followed him, as befit her role. At the same time, the room suddenly felt uncomfortably warm, the atmosphere like a pressure cooker. Her free hand itched to reach for her own weapon as a measure of protection.

As they drew closer, the three dart players stopped their game. Their laughter died. They looked Ella and Brenner up and down as the couple moved to the closed door. The men stepped aside, muttering to each other, and moved towards the bar.

"Think we've been made," Brenner whispered under his breath. He let go of Ella's hand, and she felt a momentary twinge of disappointment.

She turned the door handle and was surprised to find it unlocked. "In we go."

The door creaked on its hinges as Ella Porter and Brenner Gunn slipped inside, mostly unnoticed amidst the noise of clinking glasses and raucous laughter. She shut the door on the loudness and assessed her new surroundings. The hall was dim, lit by only a single weak bulb at the far end, its walls of unfinished pine, gray and splintering. The sweet smell of old wood mingled with that of sour beer, sticky underfoot. Ella's gaze swept the corridor, her sharp eyes hunting for any sign of Miles Cruise or his entourage.

"Remember, we're just a couple out for a drink," she murmured to Brenner, her voice barely audible. There were people back here, people up to something shady, and she didn't want to alert them to the presence of a couple of federal officers. Her heart thumped against her ribs, not from fear—Ella had long ago learned to stifle that sensation—but from the thrill of the chase.

"Right behind you, Porter," Brenner's handsome features were set in a stoic mask, but Ella noted the tightness around his eyes, a small window into the tension he carried.

The narrow hallway stretched before them, shrouded in shadows. The feeble light outlined the grimy walls and the grit on the floor. Ella's pulse quickened as she eased forward. Despite the murky surroundings, clarity sharpened her senses, honing her focus on the task at hand.

Brenner, too, moved like a panther, neither his feet nor his breathing breaking the silence that enveloped them.

She took another step, her boots whispering against the floor, avoiding an abandoned beer bottle, an empty potato chip bag, and scraps of paper. The bare bulb illuminated a half open door, the handle of a mop leaning out.

They reached a turn in the hall just beyond the bare bulb. Ella peered around the corner. Here the floor was cracked brown linoleum, covered in muddy footprints. Large antlers marked the top of the only door, at the far end.

She thrust back against the wall and caught Brenner's arm before he could round the corner. He went still. They counted three breaths and heard nothing. She nodded. Now he too peered at what had given her pause.

At the end of the hall, to the left of the antlered door, a man sat sprawled in a large, tatty blue wingback chair that seemed to swallow his form: a sentinel guarding the gateway. A sleepy sentinel – they could hear the soft whistle of a snore. At his feet, a massive dog, its coat a mottled shade of gray and black, mirrored its master's vigilance—head across his master's shoes, eyes closed, snuffling. A chain tethered him to a ring in the floor in front of the chair.

"Damn," Brenner muttered under his breath, his gaze locked on the hulking canine. "That's not just any mutt. When he wakes up . . ."

Ella's eyes flickered toward Brenner, reading the set of his jaw, the subtle shift in weight as he prepared for what came next. She knew that look, had seen it in countless briefings and operations where words became superfluous. He had a plan.

"Stay here. Keep an eye out." Brenner's voice was barely above a whisper but with an edge of command that brooked no argument. His eyes held hers for a moment—oceans of resolve, and then, so fast she thought she hadn't seen clearly – a wink. He turned back the way they had come.

She watched him stoop, his hand closing around the neck of the beer bottle next to the skirting board. The label was peeling, but the bottle glimmered murky gold in the low light.

Brenner unscrewed the cap with an adept twist. The faint pfft of gas escaping the bottle made Ella tense, but the figure at the end of the hall remained still, in dreamland. The dog snuffled again, turning on its back. Its back legs paddled the air, running in a dream hunt. Ella would have laughed, but the canine's fangs, visible despite its lolling tongue, kept her quiet.

She turned and watched as Brenner upended the bottle, letting the contents cascade down over his jacket. The liquid darkened the fabric instantly. The sharp tang of hops and barley filled the corridor.

Brenner took a deep breath, then dropped his shoulders, getting into character. He reeled around the corner, humming. She recognized the tune. It was a rude sea shanty.

The dog roused immediately, jumping to its feet, straining on its chain and growling at the intruder. Now the guard, too, jerked awake with a snort, his legs kicking out. “Down boy! Stop it!”

Then he saw Brenner tottering down the hall.

The watchman surged to his feet. He wasn’t tall, but he was broad like a sailor, dressed in jeans and a maroon flannel shirt with the sleeves rolled to the elbows, revealing forearms covered in tattoos. His hair and voice were spiky. “You! Where the hell do you think you’re going! You’re not allowed back here!”

With each step Brenner exaggerated his limp, holding the wall for balance. The corridor seemed to narrow as he passed, the shadows shrinking back against the walls.

"Hey, friend," Brenner waved, waving the beer bottle. He hiccupped. "A little help?" He grinned foolishly, his eyes unfocused, and hummed another bar.

The dog snarled, ears perked and eyes like polished coal. As she watched from the shadows, Ella could feel the animal's suspicion, a primal recognition of a predator in sheep's clothing. The guard seemed to feel it too, for he bent and unclasped the dog chain from the floor. When he straightened, he pulled the links hand over hand, dragging the animal back to his side. Its growls crescendoed.

"Easy now," Brenner stopped to sag against the wall. He took a swig from his bottle to give the dog time to settle. Some of the alcohol dribbled down his chin. His features looked blurred with drink, but Ella knew his eyes saw everything.

"Lost your way, buddy?" The guard snapped. "Go back where you came from. Now."

"Party got wild," Brenner slurred, chuckling. "And now I gotta take a leak." He needed to close the distance, to get within arm's reach before the dog decided to act.

The stench of stale beer wafted from Brenner's drenched jacket as he staggered forward. The guard's nose twitched in distaste, but his hard expression showed something between amusement and contempt for the man in front of him. "Whoa there, big guy," he warned, his voice a gravelly contrast to the muffled bass pulsing from the bar's main room. "Time to turn around."

Brenner squinted. "Jus' lookin' for the...uh...little sailor's room, ya know?" He let out an unsteady snigger, his hand reaching out to a wall that wasn't there.

"The head's the other way," the guard snapped. He allowed the dog more lead. "You hear me? The other way."

"Ah, c'mon man," Brenner drawled, offering a lopsided grin as he stumbled closer. "I'm jus' tryna find my sea legs. Is that the john there?" He pointed at the door below the antlers.

The guard shifted, the floor groaning under his weight like an old ship bracing against a storm. The amusement was gone. He jerked the dog's chain. "What's your game?" The dog growled, low and long.

"Game?" Brenner repeated, tilting his head in bewilderment. "There's no game, friend. Jus' lost is all."

Skepticism curled the guard's lips into a sneer. "You're about to find trouble. I'm gonna count to three. One. Two--"

"Look," Brenner slurred, stepping just a fraction closer. "I ain't meanin' to cause a ruckus. I jus' wanna—"

"Three!" The guard reached his right hand behind him, into the chair, inching towards something unseen, something dangerous.

"Guess we're doing this the hard way," Brenner sighed. As the guard dove for his weapon, Brenner leaped forward with the lethal grace of a seasoned combatant. His right fist shot out like a piston. "Sorry pal," he added almost apologetically as his knuckles connected with the guard's jaw.

The guard's eyes rolled back and his body went limp, crumpling over his chair. His hand released the dog chain.

The dog lunged for Brenner's throat. Brenner sidestepped as though sparring in a dojo, and the dog hit the wall. Brenner came up, scooping up the chain as he did so. Using the beast's momentary surprise to advantage, Brenner hauled the chain up short so he controlled the dog's head. It snarled and clawed at the air, but Brenner, chest heaving, held him away. The dog coughed and growled, to no avail. Brenner kept the chain tight, trooping the struggling mutt back towards Ella and the nearby supply closet.

She kicked the closet door wide to help him out and ducked aside.

The closet was a tight space, with not only the mop and bucket, but shelves stuffed with paper towels, linens, and cleaning supplies. The tang of ammonia hung in the air. Brenner tossed the mop aside and booted the bucket deep into the closet. With space cleared, Brenner frog-marched the dog inside, flung the chain in after it and slammed the door shut. He grabbed the mop and wedged its staff through the closet's metal handles.

The dog snarled and flung itself against its prison. The doors shook. But the makeshift lock held.

"Sorry, boy," Brenner muttered, patting the door as the dog walloped it again, "but you're not the one I'm here for."

The answer was a confused whimper, more like a child than a full grown attack dog.

"Gotcha," Brenner exhaled, a wry smile tugging at the corner of his mouth.

Ella was already at his side. "Nice one," she said admiringly. "You have a way with animals – and security guards." Behind the door, the dog yelped and slammed into something. Next thing they heard rolls of paper towels falling off the shelves, and the dog scrambling around in panic, clattering into mops and brooms.

"Thank you kindly," he said, smiling into her eyes, his own very blue.

Ella looked away. "You stink," she added, wrinkling her nose at the beery stench still wafting from his jacket.

He wiggled his eyebrows in her direction. Ella stifled another laugh. They began moving towards the antler door again, stepping softly. "I'm surprised no one heard our commotion," she observed, sotto voice. "It wasn't your quietest performance."

The guard still lay insensible across the arm of his chair as they approached the door. His gun lay half exposed from the cushion. Brenner picked it up, checked the safety was on, and pocketed it.

They put their ears to the door. They heard nothing but the dog, still scrabbling against his makeshift jail.

Brenner was just easing the knob open when they heard a sudden clattering behind it, the sound of a fire door yanked open to bang against the wall. A blast of cold air almost slammed the door in Brenner's hand shut, but his shoulder caught the weight of the wood. A sudden burst of men's voices filled the room beyond.

Ella stared through the crack in the door. She could only see one wall, and the back of a cluster of men. What she saw told her the room wasn't really a meeting place.

It was an armory, covered floor to ceiling with weapons. And much of the arsenal wasn't for hunting game.

They were weapons of war--for killing humans.

Chapter 5

Brenner saw what she saw. His lips formed the word, "Hell."

Both adjusted positions to see better.

A group of five men stood clustered in a semi-circle in front of the back double doors, now closed against the chill night. The armaments wall took up space to the left of the doors, aerial maps of the Seward Peninsula hung to the right. From perches on high, heads of a polar bear, a grizzly, a white wolf and an elk glowered over the maps. Aside from these, no effort had been made to update the décor. The floor was bare, pitted cement tracked with muddy footprints, and the paint on the walls was dingy and peeling. There were no windows.

The men's appearance posed a contrast to their grimy surroundings. All wore first-class heavy winter hunting gear. Thick coats adorned with fur-lined hoods framed their faces, and she saw several wearing trousers like her father used to own, thousands of dollars a pair, fur-lined yet flexible. Luxe leather gloves peeked out of pockets; earth colored cashmere scarves protected necks. All had fresh skin, like outdoorsmen, but their expensively styled haircuts and soft hands evidenced life in a board room and hinted that their outdoor look came from a spa. Ella couldn't see their eyes, but she could sense their excitement, like that of young bobcats about to prowl on their first big hunt.

By contrast, the seeming leader of the group, the one around whom they clustered, wore a worn leather jacket patched with remnants of old adventures. A scraggly silver beard framed his face, reddened from years outdoors. Broken veins left trails across his nose and cheeks. His hands, raised to gather the group's attention, were huge and calloused, the hands of a real life-long hunter among this group of players at hunting. He grinned, a guru before acolytes.

"Now you're all paid up, it's time to set the ground rules." He hefted a bear rifle from the wall to his shoulder.

As the men turned to watch him, Ella had a chance to glance at the profile of each. None matched the appearance of Miles Cruise.

And yet judging by their get-up and clandestine gathering, Ella and Brenner were in the right spot.

Ella and Brenner remained in the hall, near the unconscious guard. The barking hound was getting louder, though, as the beast protested its new confines.

Silver Beard spoke again. "Alright. Got your attention. Now listen closely. This is crucial."

His audience leaned forward.

The bearded man chuckled. "Don't. Get. Shot."

His listeners laughed, hands loaded with gold signet rings glinting as they slapped each other's shoulders.

"Alright, let's go!" Silver Beard strode through the exit door, his black leather duster flapping against his legs like the wings of a raven. The rest of the men followed him out, into an icy alley off the Nome harborside road. Ella could see a sliver of night sky above the low warehouse across the alley.

The lanky leader smoothed his beard and looked up the alley to his right. He waved his hand and his companions moved off to the left, giving him room.

"Five of them," Brenner murmured, leaning closer.

"Looks like they're not here for the local brew," Ella whispered back. She was aware of her heart pounding, both in triumph that they had found a clue to the poaching, and in anticipation of making a next move.

"Why are they milling around? Are they expecting someone?" Brenner wondered.

"More like something." Ella's fingers tightened around the grip of her gun, the chill metal a solid promise beneath the fabric of her jacket.

Outside, the men huddled briefly, their heads bowed together as if sharing a secret. As they dispersed, slipping into the alley shadows, the rumble of a vehicle ended the silence. Its headlights illuminated the shabby backstreet with its upmarket hunters, all hefting shiny weapons. A black Jeep emerged from the gloom, its engine growling like a beast scenting quarry.

"Time to move," Ella said. Her muscles coiled, ready for action, yet she held back, knowing the importance of precision over haste. They were outnumbered and outgunned. She pulled out her phone and began punching a text commanding backup units. She and Brenner would have to tail the suspects before the arrival of reinforcements enabled them to engage. As her fingers tapped on her screen, Silver Beard hauled on the open door. A spring-loaded hinge at the top began to pull it closed.

"Go," Brenner whispered, but halted again as the Jeep's lights flashed through the exit door, briefly washing over them where they crouched. They counted to three, but no one returned from outside to investigate.

"Stay on my six." Ella darted across the cement floor, avoiding the potholes. Her resolve hardened with every step. This was what she was made for. The cold coming through the not-yet-closed door bit at her exposed skin. She caught her foot on the threshold, blocking the door from closing all the way, and looked outside. The five men headed to the right and stood by the corner of the street.

The streetlamps illuminated a new flurry of falling snow, pure and peaceful.

The Jeep had apparently driven around the block to the main drag, for it appeared there at the end of the alley. It skidded to a halt, its tires crunching on the icy mix and splattering the sidewalk with dirty slush. The engine hummed low in the quiet that followed the abrupt stop. A plume of exhaust curled up into the frigid air, mingling with the darkness.

"Can you see who's driving?" Ella whispered, her breath visible in front of her face as Brenner joined her, their shoulders almost touching.

"Negative," he replied, his gaze fixed on the tinted windows of the vehicle.

Ella squinted, trying to penetrate the opaque windshield, but it was futile—the driver remained an enigma, only a shadow shifted in the vehicle, safe in anonymity. It was as if the very essence of Nome's dark underbelly had materialized in that driver's seat, mocking them.

The bar's back exit remained propped open by Ella's hand, spilling a sliver of light across the icy asphalt in the alley. Ella's breath hitched as the six men approached the Jeep, shrouded in their big coats and low-brimmed hats. Metal on their firearms gleamed dully.

"Looks like we're not the only ones who came prepared," The facetious edge in Brenner's voice masked neither his trepidation as he calculated odds, nor his resolution to act regardless of the threat.

"Too prepared," Ella agreed, eyes narrowing as she took in the scene. Her heart drummed. Like Brenner, she would not back down. But what if she failed, as she had with her father? She could almost feel Priscilla's scornful shadow lurking over her shoulder, the specter of her twin's animosity a cold reminder of the stakes.

"Stay sharp, Porter." Brenner's hand gripped her arm, bringing her back to the grubby side street. "Thoughts clear?"

"Crystal."

"Good." He gave a slight nod, his eyes never leaving the group. His limp had been forgotten, replaced by the stillness of a tracker.

A second Jeep had pulled up. The six men divided, some climbing into one, some into the other.

And then, with a burst of life, the Jeeps roared into motion. Headlights flared as they swung around, spinning slush and snow into the air.

"Damn it!" Brenner cursed, pushing out the door to the wall. "Back-up's not here yet."

"Then we can't let them get away."

"Move!" Brenner barked, already breaking cover. Ella's hesitancy dissolved completely as they raced from shadow to shadow, the Jeep's taillights their quarry. By the time they reached the main road, it was several hundred yards gone. They swerved across the street, heading for Brenner's car. Ella was out ahead.

"Backup better be close," Ella panted over her shoulder, the cold air stabbing her lungs. She could hear Brenner's steady breaths behind her, despite his uneven, loping run. She realized that his steadiness seemed the only constant in the maelstrom of her life.

"Let's just focus on tailing them," he gritted out between strides. "We lose sight, we lose everything."

With the Jeeps' red glow burning into the night, there was nothing left but the chase.

The slop of slush beneath their boots put Ella's nerves on edge, each step an obstacle to catching the Jeeps. They reached the unassuming sedan parked under the halo of a streetlamp. The car's black paint job swallowed the weak light.

"Keys!" Brenner stretched out his hand.

Ella fumbled briefly in her coat pocket before pressing the cold metal into his palm. No sooner had she done so than Brenner had the car roaring to life, the sound jarring against Nome's sleeping streets. Like the Jeep beforehand, he skidded through a U-Turn to pick up the chase.

"Steady, we need to stay invisible," Ella's mind raced as fast as her heart. The luminescent dials of the dashboard cast an eerie glow on her features, emphasizing her decided chin and thinned lips.

"Got it." Brenner shifted gears with practiced ease. His gaze flicked to the rearview mirror, then back to the road where the Jeep's taillights were a pair of dying stars in the distance.

"Turn the headlights off, as soon as we're out of this residential zone," Ella instructed. She couldn't afford a mistake, they had to get closer without being seen.

"Risky." Brenner's reply was gruff, but she caught the edge of respect.

Ella leaned forward, squinting through the darkness. The Jeeps seemed to be moving erratically, as if their drivers were unsure of their way. Her hands clenched and unclenched on her knees.

"Remember, Brenner, we can't spook them," she said, her breath fogging up the windshield. "They're armed. They'll be like cornered animals—dangerous."

"Cornered animals don't know I've hunted bigger game," he retorted.

The hum of the engine melded with the rushing wind as Ella's fingers danced over her phone, illuminated by its harsh blue glow against the night. "Dispatch, this is Agent Porter. We're in active pursuit, heading south on Seward Street. Suspects are in two black Jeeps. One's license plate ends in 4-3-Charlie. Request immediate backup."

"Copy that, Agent Porter. What's your current—"

"Close to the outskirts," she cut in, her gaze fixed on the taillights ahead. "They're not slowing down. I need units ready for a roadblock on the main exit routes out of Nome. These guys are armed and dangerous."

"Understood. Ordering roadblocks now. Be advised, backup is en-route but ETA is fifteen minutes."

"Roger that." Ella's thumb ended the call, her heart throttling against her sternum. Fifteen minutes could be fifteen too many.

Beside her, Brenner's knuckles whitened on the wheel as he made another sharp turn, the car's tires chewing through compacted snow. They couldn't afford to lose sight of their quarry.

"Roadblock's going up. But we can't count on it alone." Ella's breath fogged the window, the ghost of her anxiety visible in the air.

"Never do," Brenner muttered. Even with headlights off, his eyes were like an eagle's, scanning the road ahead for twists and obstacles. They began to gain on their quarry.

Ella chewed the inside of her cheek, pondering their next move. The chase had narrowed their world to this single strip of icy asphalt, threading through desolate terrain. The Jeep seemed to sense their presence, accelerating with renewed purpose.

"Damn it!" She hit the dashboard with a frustrated fist. "We have to keep them from reaching the open roads."

"Pushing them towards the coast could work. Trap them between the sea and the roadblock." Brenner's profile was rigid in the dim light.

"Good call." Approval warmed Ella's tone, her mind jumping ahead of the Jeep's red taillights, plotting the outcome of what they would attempt.

"Alright, then let's herd these bastards directly into a net." Brenner's voice, usually so calm, roughened with eagerness to put their plan in action. It matched the pounding of Ella's pulse.

"Net's only as good as the hunters who set it," she reminded herself.

A few snow-laden pines blurred past, a ghostly panorama against the night as Ella's hands tightened on her knees. The

SUV's tires skated over fresh powder. He turned on the car's fog lights.

"Watch the bend!" Ella snapped, over the noise of the engine.

Brenner nodded, downshifted and steered into the curve.

Ella's breath hitched as they negotiated another sharp turn, the snow kicking up behind them like a bridal train. It wasn't just about upholding the law or safeguarding wildlife; it was about protecting the people of Nome from the fallout of crime. Priscilla's scathing comments about Ella playing hero echoed in her mind; but this wasn't about heroics—it was about duty.

"Backup should be setting up the roadblock by now," Brenner said, breaking into her thoughts. "We just need to keep that Jeep pointed in the right direction."

"Right." Ella exhaled, funneling her thoughts to the next steps. There was no room for error, not when lives hung in the balance. And yet, she couldn't shake the gnawing fear of the unknown variables, the possible outcomes branching off into darkness like the tributaries of a frozen river.

"Stay on them, Brenner. You've got this!" She was talking to herself as much as to him. A sudden movement caught her eye. "Hold on!"

A moose had stepped into the road, its rack a huge crown. Ella braced herself as Brenner swerved onto the shoulder of the road to avoid the animal. He swerved again to regain the road and hit a patch of black ice. The sedan slid, donuting once before Brenner straightened her out.

When Ella remembered to breathe again, she saw that the Jeeps' taillights were still within sight, challenging them to keep up.

"Look," Brenner said suddenly, pointing ahead where the Jeep's brake lights flared red against the snow. "They're slowing down."

"Could be a trick," Ella assessed quickly. "Or maybe they've realized they're running out of road."

"Either way, now's our chance." Brenner's voice held an edge of anticipation.

"Let's hope it's the roadblock and not something worse."

First one, then the other Jeep's taillights suddenly vanished as they dipped into a depression in the landscape, and for a moment, the night swallowed them whole. Brenner leaned forward, peering through the darkness, searching for any sign of the vehicles they pursued.

"Where the hell—" he started, but cut off as the Jeeps re-emerged, cresting the rise like lions on a ridge. Engines roared, echoing across the snow-covered tundra that stretched out around them.

And then, suddenly, ahead of the Jeeps, Ella saw blue flashing lights lacerate the darkness where the sky met the horizon. The roadblock was in place a quarter mile ahead. The Jeeps began to slow.

Ella got on her phone to the marshals. "We can see you now. We're to your south. Send backup, I think they're going to try to turn off overland."

She was right. As soon as the Jeeps pulled to the shoulder, their passenger doors swung open. One man emerged from the first Jeep, three from the next. They stumbled up to the roadside drifts, incongruous in their fancy hunting gear.

Ella and Brenner pulled up behind. "Three are still in the cars," Brenner mused. "They might be splitting up, ditching their clients." He hit the lights now, the brights flooding the Jeeps. He struck the siren, and its wail pierced the night.

The hunting tourists jerked at the sound. All craned their heads in disbelief. Another wailing siren joined the song. Two vehicles had peeled away from the roadblock and were barreling toward their new position. As they closed in, Ella could see they were marshals' trucks.

Simultaneously, the tourist hunters threw off their weapons and sprinted across the open tundra, hollering and swearing as they went.

"Let's go after them!" Ella was already unholstering her Glock. "The others can take care of the guys in the Jeeps."

Brenner nodded. The two marshals' trucks were already pulling into position. He shifted his own vehicle into 4WD and jerked the wheel. The car jumped the shoulder and bounced onto the unforgiving terrain, following the fugitives' path.

The SUV's tires sprayed a white haze of frost in its wake. The running figures grew larger as the car got closer. When the car juddered over a rise, Ella could see the gray of the sea stretching out into eternity ahead of them. The fugitives were trapped. They could try to dodge the law enforcement vehicle and head back to surrender at the road, or they could throw themselves into the icy froth of the water crashing on the shore.

Ella unbuckled her seatbelt.

As they closed in on their targets, she rolled down her window. Gun in hand, she steadied her firing arm on the edge of the aperture. Snow blew across her arm, into the car, but she barely felt it.

"FBI!" she shouted. "Freeze!"

When the four men kept stumbling along, she took precise aim and fired a warning shot into the air, right above the escapees' heads. The sound reverberated across the barren landscape, mingling with the scream of sirens and the pounding of the ocean.

Two of the fleeing men faltered, glancing back over their shoulders. The other two kept running towards the sea. All were cornered, whether they admitted it or not.

"Hands up!" Ella's voice was louder than the snarl of the ocean, and equally fierce. "You're surrounded!"

In that moment, time seemed to stand still as the men processed their predicament. Their shoulders slumped. After a moment's hesitation, first one, then the rest slowly raised their hands in surrender.

“On the ground! Hands where I can see them!”

All four of them stumbled once, twice, and then dropped to the ground, wheezing, heads bowed, gloved hands flat on protruding tufts of grass.

Brenner brought the car to a complete halt. Ella flung open her door and jumped out into the snow. She kept her gun trained on them as she advanced, her grip steady and eyes sharp.

“Why,” said one of the men, gray-haired and wearing a Rolex, “you're just a little thing.” A smile showed professionally whitened teeth. The other men looked up and, like a pack of coyotes, quivered as though eyeing a lost lamb.

Then Brenner came up beside her, his presence a pillar of reassurance. His gun, too, was aimed and loaded.

The men's brief moment of bravado dissipated immediately. Their heads drooped again.

"Wise choice," Ella's gaze never left them as she approached. But with her partner as backup, the men remained meek. She knelt down and quickly handcuffed each one. She had two sets of cuffs in her own pockets, and Brenner tossed her two more. The men's eyes flickered with a mix of fear and disbelief, still winded from their flight as they struggled to catch their bearings.

"So boys, where's the party?" she demanded.

One of the men, a wiry figure with a gold earring and black hipster glasses, sneered at her. "Mind your own business," he spat defiantly. "I want my lawyer. I'm going to sue!"

"Suit yourself," Ella shrugged. "We can talk later." She didn't need to engage further. These men weren't going anywhere except where a law officer took them. She rose to her feet.

A shot split the night air, then another.

"That's from the road!" Brenner yelled. He swiveled, Ella along with him.

The two gray Marshal's SUV's and a sheriff's black and white had boxed in the Jeeps. The driver's door of the rear Jeep was open, and a guy in hunting gear stood handcuffed before it. But the lawmen were plunging behind their vehicles for cover.

In the front Jeep, two rifles poked out the windows.

They'd opened fire.

Chapter 6

The handcuffed man – Silver Beard, Ella now saw – grabbed the chance to run to the forward Jeep. As he got there, the back door flung open and he dove inside.

Ella Porter's heart drummed a furious rhythm against her ribs as she and Brenner dashed away from the quartet of handcuffed men sprawled on the hard-packed snow. The sharp report of gunfire reverberated again. She ducked as she scrambled over the tussocky ground, knowing that upright she would be an easy target for those high-powered weapons. She glanced at Brenner. He too had crouched, but not so low as Ella, for his injured leg had trouble with the odd position. Despite the disability, he kept pace, eyes trained on the trouble ahead.

"Keep your head down," Brenner barked, and she realized she had straightened as she looked at him.

Ella stooped lower and kept moving. A gust of wind, laden with snow, stung her face and snatched away her reply. Her fingers tightened around the grip of her service weapon, the cold metal a familiar weight through her gloves.

They hurtled forward, boots scraping over the iced grass. Up ahead, the Jeep jostled wildly as its driver attempted to back away from the roadblock onto the tundra. Ella exchanged a look with Brenner; they didn't need words.

They raised their weapons in tandem, and Ella felt the recoil jar her shoulder as she squeezed the trigger. One, two, three—sharp cracks split the air, and the Jeep's tires burst, one after another, the vehicle sagging into the snow like a wounded animal.

"Nice shooting," Brenner praised, without looking away from the disabled Jeep.

“Thank you kindly,” she quipped back.

The Jeep's engine groaned, its efforts to flee now grounded by deflated rubber. Ella and Brenner were only a few yards away.

A new crack of rifle fire pierced the night, this time aimed in their direction. A bullet whizzed past Ella's head. She flung herself behind the trunk of their own vehicle, snow kicking up around her boots.

"Dammit!" Brenner cursed from beside her. His eyes locked onto the Jeep where the three other hunters had barricaded themselves. "Ella, cover me!"

She gritted her teeth and returned fire, the reports of her gun lost in simultaneous return fire.

"FBI! Get out with your hands up!" Ella shouted, her voice hoarse against the cold wind. It was a futile command, lost in the roar of another volley from the Jeep.

She spotted a figure lying crumpled by the nearest blockade vehicle. A Marshal... she'd seen him in the briefing room. Dawes? Dawson?

The man lay on the ground, bleeding through his jacket.

"Move! Move!" The remaining marshal hollered, crouched low behind his vehicle, providing covering fire for Ella and Brenner. The sheriff's deputy had joined him.

Ella peeked from her makeshift barricade, sighting one of the gunmen through the shattered Jeep window. She squeezed the trigger. Her bullet smashed through glass and metal. The man's shout was cut off abruptly, and his raised rifle fell from his hands.

"Keep them pinned!" Brenner ordered, his voice carrying the authority of a man who had seen too many battles. He clutched his rifle, its stock snug against his shoulder.

"Left side! Left side!" Brenner's warning came just as a gunman emerged from the back passenger side of the Jeep, galloping around the bumper to flank them. It was Silver Hair, cuffs off, gun on his shoulder as comfy as a baby, eyes blank.

Ella swiveled, firing before the man could even aim.

He hit the ground, hard.

He didn't rise.

Her breath fogged in the air as she stared at him.

"Stay sharp," Brenner said, reloading his weapon with swift, sure movements. "There are more of them, and they're desperate."

By her count, two remained in the Jeep. Unless there was someone she had not spotted.

This thought ate at her, corrosive against her psyche. "Desperate people make mistakes," Ella muttered under her breath, watching the Jeep for any sign of movement.

"Let's give them a chance to make one," Brenner replied. Together, they kept the pressure on, gunfire echoing off the trees. The other Marshal and the sheriff's deputy joined the volley. Finally, Brenner held up his hand. Silence settled on the tundra, except for the rumble of the Jeep's engine.

For a few seconds, nothing and no one moved.

Then the vehicle jolted forward, roaring towards the sheriff's car.

Brenner pressed off with one sharp shot. Ella watched as the Jeep's windshield splintered, a rose window of death blossoming from its center where the driver's head had been seconds before.

"Got him," Brenner's voice betrayed no triumph.

The Jeep swayed, then stilled. Ella watched for movement, whether anyone inside remained. She heard nothing. Was it the silence of the grave, or that of trickery?

"Are they..." Ella started, her question trailing off into the brittle air.

"Either killed or they're putting on a damn good act." Brenner limped closer to the Jeep, too tired to disguise his injury. His boots on the snow had the rhythm of a drum beating a disjointed death march.

"Stay alert," Ella reminded herself. Her finger rested lightly on the trigger of her gun, ready to respond to the slightest provocation.

"Can't see a thing through those tinted windows," Brenner said, a hint of frustration seeping through. "Could be setting us up for a nasty surprise."

"Or they're hoping we'll let our guard down," Ella replied, staring at the Jeep's doors. Her mind hurdled over possibilities, each scenario ending with more blood staining the snow.

Snow crunched beneath her boots as she joined Brenner by the Jeep. The acrid smell of gunpowder mingled with the flakes still drifting down. Each step the colleagues took was measured, deliberate, echoes of training and instinct woven together into harmonized choreography.

The distance closed, two yards, then one, until they were within arm's reach of the vehicle.

Then the Jeep's passenger door burst open with violent force, slamming into Brenner's side with a dull thud. His grunt of pain was lost in the explosion of snow and motion as a figure lunged from within, pistol in hand.

The man in the passenger seat. He was bleeding, shot, but alive enough to fight like a cornered bear.

"Gun!" Ella shouted, her own weapon snapping up in an arc as natural as breathing. Brenner staggered, but his fall was arrested by the deep snow, and he twisted, trying to bring up his rifle.

The gunman's face was contorted in a snarl. He pointed the pistol at Brenner, finger tightening on the trigger.

"Down!" Ella barked, even as her mind screamed for her to take the shot. But Brenner was too close, the angles all wrong.

Time slowed, each millisecond stretching into infinity as Brenner snatched at the man's leg, yanking him into the snow. The gunshot missed as the man swiveled like a fulcrum. He slid towards Brenner, who yanked him down. They grappled on the snowy road, their bodies a blur of motion. Ella's heart raced as she sought the clean line of fire that could save Brenner, a line that refused to present itself.

Her finger hovered over the trigger, as she steeled herself for the moment when she would have to choose.

The gap finally came—an inch of space as Brenner ducked, his face concentrated on raw survival. Ella didn't hesitate; her finger squeezed the trigger in a breathless moment. The sharp report of her Glock cut through the Alaskan air.

She yelled as the gunman's body jerked from the impact of the bullet, his weapon clattering uselessly to the ground. Brenner rolled away and came up in a crouch, his eyes darting across the scene, assessing for any new threats.

Her breathing was heavy, misting in big clouds, but her hands remained steady on her gun. She returned her attention to the Jeep. Nothing moved. She edged toward the vehicle again over the crusty, blood-spattered snow.

A single gunshot from behind her fractured her concentration. She whirled just in time to see the remaining marshal lower his smoking weapon.

She turned to see that of the four men they'd left cuffed, one had been charging towards the barricade. Now he crumpled to the ground, his body etching another dark stain onto the ice and snow.

"Target down!" the marshal barked. His voice carried an edge of grim satisfaction.

Ella's chest heaved from exertion and tension. Her fingers were stiff around her firearm, the metallic taste of fear lingered. What if she had missed the shot? What if she had hit Brenner instead? She glanced back at Brenner, who gave her a solemn nod, his face also lined with strain.

Ella's gaze shifted back to the Jeep, its tires punctured and deflated, nothing more than a hulking carcass of unanswered questions. She felt a shudder pass through her as she considered the lengths these men had gone to, the lives they had discarded in their bid for escape.

"Would they really kill feds just to cover up a hunting spree?" She voiced her question aloud. "It doesn't make sense. What the hell were they transporting?"

"Who knows with these types?" Brenner holstered his sidearm. "But whatever it is, it's got to be big. Nobody shoots at marshals unless they're desperate to keep something hidden."

Ella nodded slowly, her eyes troubled. She could feel the weight of the Alaskan wilderness pressing in on her, the vast, silent witness to mankind's capacity for inhumanity. It was as though the very air she breathed was laden with secrets, each one darker than the last.

"Let's secure the scene." Brenner's voice halted her reverie. "We need to make sure there are no more surprises waiting for us."

Ella nodded and approached the Jeep. Crimson sprayed the snow around it, a modern-art canvas of death.

"Something doesn't add up here, Brenner." She drew closer to the vehicle, the metallic tang of blood sharp in her nostrils. "Why risk a war with feds?"

"Could be drugs... or—" Brenner started, but Ella was already at the Jeep's window, peering inside.

Her hand trembled as she wiped away the condensation from the glass, revealing the interior. For a moment, the world seemed to drop away. For a moment, she thought she would gag. Next second, she yanked the door open.

"Holy shit, Ella, what is it?" Brenner limped closer, but she could not respond, could not translate the shout lodged in her throat into coherent words.

Inside the Jeep, there were no bundles of illicit substances, no gleaming cache of weapons.

Instead, in the rear, there was a cage. And in that cage cowered a woman, hands covering her head.

This case wasn't just about poaching. It was about abduction.

Chapter 7

Ella Porter's breath fogged the cold glass of the viewing window at the Marshall's station, her gaze fixed on the woman huddled in a corner of the sterile room. Outside, the long night still pressed against the windows, alleviated by halos from a few weak streetlamps. The buzz of fluorescent lights overhead mixed with the murmurs of officers discussing the shootout that had left one of their colleagues in critical condition, and four perpetrators dead or wounded. The same question arose repeatedly: *What* was going on? Until now, only the occasional crackle of radio static punctuated the eerie hum. Ella felt the weight of each second ticking by.

A woman sat in the interrogation room, the center of this nocturnal vigil. Several hours before, she had been nothing more than a cringing figure in a rusted portable dog kennel. She wore jeans adorned with silver spangles and an orange silk halter, both stained and dirty. Her hair, ash blonde, was shoulder length and snarled, her hazel eyes red-rimmed. She had no coat, hat or shoes, and shivered uncontrollably. Scars pitted the flesh around her elbow, old scars, evidence of a sad past left behind.

Paramedics had treated her for exposure and minor injuries.

Now she was wrapped in the borrowed warmth of a navy blue jacket emblazoned with the local fire department's crest, with rag wool socks on her feet and a wool blanket tucked around her for good measure. The dark blue emphasized the paleness of her face. Her hands, quivering slightly, clutched a paper cup that seemed to offer more comfort than its contents could possibly hold.

"Here," Ella said softly, stepping into the room with another steaming drink, this one in a white porcelain mug to retain the heat. "I thought you might like some more hot cocoa."

The woman started, her gray-green eyes panicked as though she had expected someone else. Luckily her paper cup was almost empty, so nothing spilled. Ella gently took it in hand, giving the woman the full mug instead. The fear faded, replaced by tears.

“Thank you,” she whispered.

Ella took a seat opposite her, giving her space but staying close enough to bridge the gap of silence if needed.

"Of course," Ella replied. Ella noted the way the woman's eyes darted to the door every few minutes, the slight tremor in her fingers as they gripped the mug. Fear still held her captive in invisible chains.

"Can you tell me—?" Ella started, then caught herself. This wasn't the time for questions. Not yet. Instead, she said, "I'm Ella. I want to help you."

A nod, almost imperceptible, was the woman's only response. Ella respected her silence. She would not rush her, would not shove her into reliving whatever nightmare had locked her away in a cage in the Alaskan wilderness.

"Drink your cocoa," Ella encouraged. "It'll help warm you up."

"Okay." The woman took a small sip, her eyes closing for a moment as if savoring a brief respite from her reality.

Ella watched her. Tension knotted her own stomach. There were so many questions pressing against her lips, so many pieces of this puzzle to fit together. But patience was part of the job, part of the vow she'd taken when she joined the FBI—to serve and protect, to seek justice for those who couldn't find it on their own.

She thought of her sister Priscilla, of the blame that had driven a wedge between them. In another life, perhaps, they would have been side by side in moments like these, twin reflections of determination. But that bridge had burned long ago, leaving only ashes and regret.

"Is it always this dark here?" the woman asked suddenly, her voice barely above a whisper. She was looking at the night outside the window, not at the lamps in the room.

"Most of the winter, yeah," Ella replied, a smile tugging at her lips. "But you get used to it. The darkness makes the stars shine brighter."

"Stars," the woman echoed, a faint glimmer of wonder surfacing in her eyes.

"Once you're feeling better, I'll show you," Ella promised. "The night sky here is something else."

"Thank you," the woman said again, a little stronger this time. "For being kind."

"It's what we do," Ella responded.

The silence lengthened again. Ella spent it studying the woman's fingers. They were delicate and small, with some sort of swirled orange and red nail polish. But the nails were ripped to the quick, the polish scraped mostly away, and the fingers covered with cuts and scrapes. Clearly, she had tried to fight her way out of the cage at some point.

Ella raised her eyes to the woman's face, but the latter kept her head down, hair falling over her eyes. Gradually, however, Ella realized the fingers were not quite so tight around the cup, not quite as trembling. Ella eased her chair closer. The soft scrape of metal against linoleum disturbed the quiet.

“What's your name?” They had found no ID on the woman.

It took a moment for her to answer. "Kerry," the woman said, then more strongly, "I'm Kerry."

Ella nodded encouragingly. A strand of her own blonde hair came loose from her ponytail, and she tucked it behind her ear. "Do you have a last name?"

"Kerry Lonigan."

Ella nodded again in acknowledgement. "Ella Porter. I'm the FBI agent investigating your case."

At this Kerry looked directly at Ella, her hazel eyes wide and confused. "There's a case? I didn't think anyone even knew we were missing."

"We?" said Ella sharply. "There's someone else?" Immediately she regretted her sharp tone, because Kerry shrank back. "Forgive me, I didn't mean to snap, I'm just surprised. Who else was with you?"

"Emma," whispered Kerry, keeping her eyes down. "They took Emma too."

Ella waited a few moments to let Kerry recover, before asking her next question, gentle as kitten.

"Who is Emma? Is she family?"

"Nooo, not family. Emma found me. In Seattle. I was on the street, running away from my boyfriend. I thought I was free, but then I saw him, him and a . . .friend of his. I knew they were going to hurt me if they found me." Kerry was hugging herself, rocking on her chair. "I ducked into a coffee shop to escape and ran into Emma. She knew at once what was going on, I don't know how but she did. She whisked me out the back door and took me home. When she heard my story she said I had to come to Alaska with her. She's doing research here, something about sailors and welfare. She said we'd be safe and I would have time to make plans. And then . . ."

"And then?" Emma prompted after a few seconds.

"She got news that she got a big grant. She was over the moon after she got the letter. She wanted to celebrate, go out dancing. She got free tickets to a little club in her mailbox, some sort of prize. I didn't want to go, but she had been so good to me . . . When we got inside, we realized it wasn't a club, just a grotty bar. The bartender sent us through a door, he said the club was at the back. But *they* were waiting. One grabbed me, and held something over my mouth and nose. When I woke up, Emma was gone and I was in . . . a cage . . ." Kerry bent over nearly double, rocking herself, shuddering inside her blanket cocoon. Her cocoa sat forgotten on the table.

Ella hunkered down at eye level. "I am so sorry. I am so sorry, Kerry. I want to hold your hand, but only if that would be a comfort." She paused, wondering if she had gone too far, but not wanting to leave Kerry alone in her nightmare.

Kerry opened waterlogged eyes. She held out one shaking hand, continuing to cradle herself with the other, and clutched Ella's like a lifeline.

"Can you tell me about the men?" Ella's eyes were patient and kind, even as her questions persisted. "The ones who put you in that cage?"

Kerry let go of her hand and fixed her haunted gaze on her mug, where tendrils of steam rose like ghosts. She hugged the mug with her hands, as if its warmth could shield her from the memories. Ella watched, heart aching, as the woman's lips parted, but no words came forth. Kerry started to rock again.

"Was there something about them? Anything distinctive?" Ella prodded, leaning forward, her own hands clasped tightly in her lap to still their trembling.

As if on cue, the door creaked open, halting the conversation. Brenner Gunn stepped into the dimly lit room. His presence radiated strength despite the limp that marred his stride. Ella felt a surge of gratitude at the sight of him.

"Got something," Brenner kept his baritone voice subdued, so as not to frighten their witness. His eyes softened as they rested briefly on Kerry's trembling form, and then met Ella's for a moment. When he spoke again he addressed both of them. "Prints came back from the hunters we arrested. Two hits—ex-cons. Tax fraud and insider trading."

Ella's eyebrows lifted in silent question, absorbing the information while observing the woman's reaction. There was no flicker of recognition.

"A couple of cheaters, then," Ella commented. "Typical. They like the thrill of getting away with stuff, pretending they're important." But she filed the detail away, another piece of the puzzle to fit into place later. "Anything else?"

"Yeah. One of the drivers and Silver Beard are ex-cons too. They served time for armed robbery and aggravated assault – they were buddies."

Another pertinent scrap of information. "Thank you, Brenner," she said, her attention returning to the woman. "Kerry, this is important. These men, they might be the key to understanding what happened to you. Did they say anything to you?" Ella continued, her tone hopeful. "Anything that can help us find them?"

The woman's eyes darted between Ella and Brenner, the deer-in-headlights look giving way to something else—a glimmer of determination, perhaps.

"Killed," the word was so faint, Ella almost didn't catch it. "Th ey... talked about... killing."

"Who did they kill?" Ella leaned in, her pulse increasing.

"Others," the woman breathed out, a new tear slipping down her cheek.

"Others?" Ella echoed, her mind spinning.

A nod, slow and solemn, was the only confirmation she received.

Ella's stomach clenched tight. "Are they..." She couldn't finish the sentence, the weight of it too heavy on her tongue.

Another nod, more tears.

"Okay, okay," Ella soothed, reaching out to cover the woman's trembling hands with her own. "You're safe now."

“And Emma?” The girl rubbed the back of her hand across her eyes. “Do you think Emma is safe?”

“I don’t know. But we’ll do everything we can to find her. What does she look like?”

“Medium height, slender, a runner,” the words tumbled out. “Beautiful red-gold hair.”

“We’ll look for her,” Ella repeated, standing. “I promise.”

Beside her, Brenner's jaw set in a hard line.

Twenty minutes later, Ella was back in the interview room with Kerry. She had used the intervening time to go into the ladies’ room and slam her hand against the white tiled wall. Someone was hunting women. That was the intel that Whiler hadn't been able to share. That was the reason the FBI wanted a liaison on the case. That was the reason they wanted *her*, Ella, with the task force. Her head spun with revulsion and she hit the wall again, this time with both hands.

"Ella," Brenner called from outside. "You okay?"

"I'm fine," she lied, splashing water on her face and wiping her hands on a paper towel. She crumpled the paper and tossed it into the trash bin. That's what she would do to the monsters organizing these hunts.

Then she strode from the room. When she saw Brenner in the hallway, she pointed to glossies in his hand. "I.D. Photos?"

"Fingerprints and names." He handed them over.

Now she pushed the list of names across the table to Kerry. The slight girl was holding yet another warm mug of liquid.

"Can you tell me if you recognize any of their names?" Ella asked. She watched Kerry's eyes move slowly over the paper.

Kerry shook her head and pushed the paper back. "I don't recognize any of those names."

Ella tried another tack.

"Does the name Miles Cruise mean anything to you?" Ella's blue gaze did not waver from the other woman, trying to coax out the secrets that might lead them closer to the monsters she now knew she was hunting.

At the mention of the name, the cup nearly slipped from Kerry's grasp, sloshing hot liquid across the blanket that swaddled her. Her eyes widened and her breath hitched. She began to hyperventilate, her whole body wracked. It was as if the name had flipped a switch inside her.

Ella's own heart skipped a beat as she caught the reaction. "Please," Ella urged, resting her hand near the woman's, offering a silent promise of security. "Anything you can tell us about him could help."

The woman's lips parted slightly, her chest juddering with each inhalation as if she was bracing herself to dive into horror. Ella knew at once that whatever Kerry said would be important.

She watched with bated breath as the woman drew another shuddering breath, her fingers trembling around the mug that now sat cold on the table.

"Miles Cruise," the woman whispered, her voice a mere thread in the air. "He... he was there."

"Who is Miles Cruise to you?" Ella probed softly, her eyes locking onto the woman's wide ones, seeking not just answers but understanding.

"From Seattle ..." The woman's voice cracked, and she swallowed hard, visibly struggling to form the words. "He is . . . was . . . my boyfriend."

Ella leaned forward, straining to hear.

Kerry's eyes looked back into nightmare. "He's the one Emma wanted to get me away from. He wants me dead. He wants us all dead."

"All?" Ella echoed, her thoughts racing to piece together a mosaic of unspeakable deeds from shards of fractured testimony.

The woman nodded, a tear streaking down her cheek, shimmering in the harsh fluorescent light. "Others," she breathed out, her gaze distant, as if lost in the labyrinth of her own harrowing memories. "He beat me, said it was my fault because I was bad. Then I found there were others. Women. He did worse than beat them. I saw photographs." She pressed her hands hard against her eyelids, and the blanket slid from her shoulders to the floor.

"What did Miles Cruise do to these women that was worse than beating?" Ella asked, her voice steady despite the dread clawing at her insides.

"Killed them," came the almost inaudible confession. "I saw... I saw it happen. Or... I saw him take them, and put them into a truck, and take them into the backcountry. And when he came back, he came back with only the empty cages. He was...

hunting them." She was rocking again now, and the words came out as a moan. Her eyes met Ella's, and in them, the FBI agent recognized someone who had stared into the darkest corners of humanity.

"Hunted them," Ella repeated internally. This was far worse than she had imagined. "Where were you when this happened?"

"Trapped," the woman replied, a shiver running through her despite the warmth of the jacket enveloping her frame. "In a cage... like an animal." Her voice broke, but she forged on, compelled by a survivor's need to bear witness. "I couldn't stop him."

"Nobody's blaming you," Ella assured her. She needed to keep the woman talking, to extract every clue that could lead them to this monster.

The woman across from her, pale and fragile as a winter bloom, nodded but not in assent. Her eyes, large and brimming with unshed tears, held Ella's gaze with a haunting steadiness. "I blame myself," she said. "I blame myself for Emma. And now I know she's dead," she continued, her voice so faint it seemed the very air between them carried the weight of her words. "Dead. Like all of them."

"Do you know where?"

"No." Kerry's fingers plucked at the blanket. "But I'm sure I was supposed to find out tonight. B-but... I think I know how *you* can find them."

Kerry's fingers continued to tremble as they reached toward the hem of her jeans. She lifted the fabric, revealing a slender ankle encircled by a metal bracelet, its surface dull and unassuming in the fluorescent light of the room. But it was what lay beneath that caught Ella's attention—a black device, no larger than a silver dollar, adhered tightly against her skin.

"Is that...?" Ella couldn't finish the question, as the implications dawned on her.

"A tracker," the woman supplied, her voice gaining a measure of strength as though the act of sharing her burden lightened it ever so slightly. "So he always knew where we were."

Ella's thoughts tumbled over each other like cascading dominos. A tracker. He must have considered his victims his property. And if he tracked her... The realization hit her with the force of a freight train. "The others?" Ella probed. "The other women. Did they have trackers like this one?"

Kerry gave a little nod from where she huddled in her blanket. "I think so," she whispered. "Bound and... tagged. It wasn't a fair hunt. There wasn't any escape."

Ella's heart clenched at the thought—women reduced to quarry in a sick game. She pictured them, each with an identical metal shackle, their hunters tracking them wherever they went.

"May I take a closer look?" Ella asked gently, reaching toward the device. The woman hesitated, then inched her leg forward slightly, allowing Ella to examine it.

The tracker was a grim thing; cold, unfeeling technology used for a sinister purpose. Ella's fingers traced the outline of the device, feeling the edges where metal met skin. A shiver ran down her spine, but not from the chill of the Alaskan night seeping into the station.

"If we can track your signal," Ella started, her voice steady amid the whirlwind of thoughts, "there's a chance we can find the others." Her blue eyes, so similar to Cilla's, showed resolve rather than vengeance.

"Does it... Does it hurt?" Brenner's voice broke through, concern wrapped in each word.

The woman shook her head minutely and whispered, "Not anymore."

"Good. That's good," Brenner said, clearly at a loss for how to offer better comfort. He shifted his gaze to Ella. "We can use this."

Ella stood, rolling her shoulders back to release some tension. "We'll be right back," she assured Kerry.

The woman nodded. She still looked fragile, but less alone.

Brenner joined Ella at the door, where they conferred quietly. "Let's get our tech team on this immediately," Ella said. "They might be able to isolate the frequency of the tracker, or whatever signal it's emitting. Then we can get out there and find these women. And their murderers."

Chapter 8

The rotor blades sliced through the dense Alaskan night, a symphony of whirring and chopping above the silent wilderness. The blackness was so absolute it seemed to swallow the helicopter whole as they hovered over the vast stretch of snow and trees. Inside the aircraft's cabin, Ella Porter's eyes were fixed on the glowing screen of Brenner Gunn's SAT phone, her blonde hair tied back in a functional ponytail that swayed with each tilt of the aircraft.

"Damn it," Brenner muttered, his broad frame tensed against the vibrations of their aerial steed. "We should be seeing three signals."

Ella leaned closer, squinting at the screen where only one blinking dot persisted in its lonely dance. Her heart squeezed tight in her chest, mirroring the clutch of her hand around the handset. She knew the vast white canvas below held secrets just out of reach.

She still pictured that ankle monitor, wrapped tightly around Kerry's leg. Had she been telling the truth? Were there others out there? It seemed too monstrous to believe.

And yet, they'd been able to track the transponder's signal, and now found themselves racing towards the blinking dot visible on the screen.

"Are you sure this is working right?" she asked, her voice barely audible above the roar of the engine.

"It's military-grade tech," Brenner shouted back, his gaze glued to the screen. "It doesn't make mistakes."

"Then why one signal?" Ella pressed on, her brows furrowing. The worry gnawed at her, an insatiable beast. "Kerry mentioned at least three women unaccounted for."

"Interference? Broken transmitters?" Brenner suggested. His answer did little to reassure her.

"Or something worse," Ella whispered more to herself than to him. Her mind spun wild scenarios, each grimmer than the last.

"Could be they're together," Brenner offered, shifting to get a better view out the window. "Would explain one signal."

"Right." Ella nodded, though her gut twinged with doubt. She knew the unforgiving nature of the Alaskan wilderness; it didn't take prisoners—it consumed them. And somewhere down there lay the answers they sought, shrouded in mystery and ice.

Brenner reached over and gave her shoulder a squeeze, the gesture stirring warmth in her chest despite the cold dread that had settled in her bones. She was glad he was along.

"Let's find our missing women, Porter. We don't need to think about anything else now."

"I want to find them alive," Ella asserted grimly, staring out into the abyss. The single, persistent GPS signal on the screen seemed to mock her, a lodestone drawing them towards one answer when she really wanted another.

It was still dark, even though it was six o'clock in the morning. The sun wouldn't rise for another four hours. Instead, a searchlight cast its restless gaze over the untamed tundra. Thousands of acres of grassland butted up against occasional regiments of snow draped pines. At times the searchlight revealed a thread of road or river, or slopes which disappeared into shadow. Ella knew that when daylight came, the mountains hulking in darkness would loom around them.

"Storm's rolling in fast from the west," the pilot's voice cut through the thrum of the rotors, gruff with concern. "Visibility's gonna be shot to hell."

Ella's breath fogged the glass as she leaned closer to the window, tracking the spotlight's path. She knew the pilot wanted them to turn back and seek shelter, pick up the search another day. But retreat was a luxury they couldn't afford—not with possible lives hanging in the balance. She didn't react to fear the same way most did. As a self-described adrenaline junkie, Ella had thrown herself into harsh and inclement conditions to do her work. Now was no exception.

"Keep going," Ella commanded, resisting the pilot's anxiety. "We can't lose them. Not now."

Brenner gave her a curt nod, then returned to his tracking. He understood the stakes, the razor-thin line between a rescue and a recovery mission.

"Porter, I've seen storms like this turn in minutes," the pilot persisted. "It's your call, but—"

"I've made the call. We press on." Ella interjected. Her fingers curled into fists, nails digging into her palms as if to anchor herself against the doubt in the cabin and the storm without.

"Then hold on tight," the pilot conceded, adjusting the controls as the first gusts of wind buffeted the aircraft. The helicopter shuddered, a prelude to a rough symphony.

Ella exchanged a look with Brenner, finding a reflection of her own resolve mirrored in his eyes.

"Come on," she murmured under her breath, a silent prayer to the God that watched over this frozen expanse. "Give us something."

The rotors continued their beat, their rhythm more erratic as they tussled with the wind that beat the fuselage. The helicopter pitched and yawed, each gust a fresh challenge to its dominance of the skies.

"Shit," Brenner muttered, his voice barely audible over the din. "This is no weather for flying."

From the cockpit, the pilot's strained voice crackled through the headsets. "I'm trying to keep her steady, but this storm isn't playing fair. Keep your eyes peeled. Two minutes, then we're heading back. No questions."

Ella didn't bother arguing.

The beam from the searchlight was a narrow escape from the clutches of darkness, revealing only fragments of the Alaskan wilderness below. Ella looked and looked, but saw nothing.

"Over there!" Brenner shouted suddenly, pointing towards the margin of the light. It was a fleeting hint of blue amidst the snow, like the memory of the sky on a clear day.

"Can you get us closer?" Ella called to the pilot, staring at the anomaly.

"Attempting to," came the terse reply. The helicopter banked, tilting precariously as it fought the tempest.

The blue marker became clearer, the corner of large tarp flapping like an untied sail. Ella's breath caught in her throat as she leaned forward, straining her eyes against the snow kicked up by the wind.

"Damn, that's got to be something," Brenner said, his hand absentmindedly massaging his thigh. Sitting cramped for so long aggravated his old injury, even beneath layers of warm clothing.

"Could be anything," Ella replied, but hope sparked within her. The tarp wasn't nature's creation; it was a sign of human presence, a sign of life. It could be a shelter, a makeshift tent. Or a banner, identifying a need for help. Her mind raced, conjuring scenarios of the missing women, alive or—

"Keep it together, Porter," she chided herself silently. "Focus on the facts, not the what-ifs."

"Looks secured to something," Brenner observed, squinting into the spotlight's glare. A sniper's eyes missed little, even in these conditions.

"Ground team's gonna have one hell of a time getting to that in this storm," the pilot remarked, though his tone suggested he shared their curiosity.

"Then let's make sure they don't waste their time. We need to know what's under that tarp."

As the pilot guided the copter down, each downdraft and cross-wind threatened to tip it. It rode towards the ground like a boat riding a hurricane's waves. The pilot's forearms bulged and sweat glistened on his face as he worked to hold the machine steady. But for Ella, the fear of not knowing whether the women lived or died was far worse than any storm.

"Almost there," Brenner confirmed, holding onto his seat with both hands. Another blast of wind shook the chopper, almost sending it scudding into some trees before the pilot gained control again.

"Ready," Ella echoed. The helicopter wasn't, but she was.

The helicopter edged closer, and the blue tarp loomed larger, a defiant flag in the face of the storm, marking the spot where truth waited to be unearthed.

"Can you set us down?" Ella had to shout to cut through the roar of the rotors and the gale.

"Negative," the pilot shouted back over comms. "No safe LZ in sight. It's a no-go for landing."

“We can’t fly past this. We have to get down there.”

The helicopter shuddered, buffeted by another gust that snatched at its skids. The spotlight was right on the tarp now.

"Hover then," she commanded, her gaze fixed on the landscape rolling beneath them. "We go down on lines."

"Are you out of your mind?" Brenner grabbed her hands, the calluses on his evidence of his own difficult life. "Ella, it's a damn blizzard out there!"

"Then we brace for a damn blizzard." Her retort left no room for argument, her FBI training surfacing with authoritative ease. Blue eyes mirrored the storm's ferocity, even as she gripped his hand more tightly. "I can't let this go, Brenner. Not when we're this close."

He studied her, the storm outside rivaled by the one he saw within her. “Okay,” he conceded. “Let’s do it then.” He let go of her and turned aside to ready their gear.

A few minutes later, the pilot fought to keep the aircraft steady as Ella and Brenner, geared up, moved to the edge of the open door. Snowflakes invaded the cabin, stinging their faces, reminding them of the raw wilderness awaiting them.

"Jump on three!" Brenner yelled, his eyes locked on hers, offering a silent promise to see this through together.

"One. Two. Three!" Ella counted, and they plunged into the abyss.

The world transformed into a maelstrom of white as they descended, the wind swinging them back and forth like a punching bag. Snow blinded her, so Ella let the rope guide her descent, her hands operating the harness through muscle memory.

Brenner's shadow stayed beside her, a ghost warrior in the squall. They hit the ground hard, knees bending to absorb the impact, their bodies instantly engulfed by the cold embrace of the wilderness.

"We've got to move!" she gasped, her breath crystalizing in the air.

They unhooked themselves from the lines and staggered toward the tarp, each step a duel against the elements. The storm seemed to echo the chaos in Ella's mind—questions swirling like the snow around them, doubts piercing like the ice underfoot.

She thought of Priscilla, of the rift between them... Thoughts of her sister kept gnawing at her like the cold to her bones. She couldn't say why.

"Stay close!" Brenner shouted, though he was only a few feet away.

Ella's boots swished through the new snow as they made their way to the tarp, her eyes squinting against the flurries that whipped her face. Brenner was right behind her, his big form a shelter against the wind.

"Ready?" she asked, not sure if her voice was loud enough.

"Let's do this."

Her hands, tingling with cold even in her fur-lined gloves, were steady as she grasped the corner of the tarp. The blue fabric was incongruous here, a splash of color against the endless white, like Priscilla's sea-shell earrings against the backdrop of their bleak childhood home. Tent pegs seemed to be holding the tarp in place, keeping three corners tight to the ground.

Brenner joined her in pulling at the frozen pegs. The blue material resisted as if it wanted to keep its secret hidden. With a final tug, the truth lay bare.

The sight struck Ella, a punch to the gut that robbed her of breath and almost doubled her over.

It now made sense why there hadn't been three signals from three locations.

The truth lay evident before them: Three women, their bodies frozen in tableau, a grotesque slumber party. From each, the shaft of an arrow protruded, a hunter's arrow.

Ella gasped for air but forced herself not to look away. The sight before her was like something out of a horror film, but what she saw was real, not cosmetics and special effects. The women's bodies were frozen, limbs at awkward angles, not resting peacefully. Their expressions, too, were frozen – in terror. They had not died painlessly.

The wind dropped, but the snow increased. Thick clumps fell across the women, covering them in shrouds of pure white, as if nature itself wanted to rectify the violations perpetrated here. Snow also blanketed bloodstains around the bodies, covering the obscenity with ethereal beauty. Even three surrounding trees donned white, holy sentries around an open mass grave.

Ella's eyes went back to the arrows. Snow caught in the fletching, and frost glistered on the shafts. The arrows were important, she knew. She just didn't know why yet.

She forced herself to look at each woman's face. She owed them that at least. A blonde, a brunette, and, oh, dear heaven, a woman with copper gold hair in a silk party blouse. With limbs outflung, each woman seemed to be trying to tell their stories. Their clothes were tattered, arms and faces scratched. The blond, with spiked hair and overplucked brows, clutched a silver necklace adorned with intricate carvings, its chain tarnished by the elements.

Brenner stood beside her, his expression mirroring her own sickening horror. The silence between them felt heavy, each lost in their own thoughts.

"God," Brenner exhaled. "Who does something like this?"

"Someone who thinks a human life is just a trophy to take," Ella said, her throat tight with revulsion. This was no poacher's random act; it was calculated, planned, carried out, meticulous.

She knelt beside the closest body, that of the brunette, noting details—the pallor of the skin, the way the ice crystals clung to eyelashes, the expression forever locked in time. She reached out, hesitated, then tried to close the woman's staring eyes with a gentle touch. It didn't work. The skin was too frozen. The hunters had denied her even this small dignity.

Snow whipped around them, blinding and disorienting. Ella barely noticed.

"Storm's picking up!" the pilot's voice crackled over the comm. "We have to leave now!"

"Understood!" Brenner shouted back, gripping Ella's arm to guide her. She wanted to pull away. It didn't feel right leaving the women here... all alone and defiled.

But they'd located the bodies. And if they downed their chopper, they'd be of little use to anyone.

She shot a final glance back towards the frozen bodies, taking a snapshot in her mind.

And then she trudged back to the trailing ropes and the groaning mechanical beast waiting to lift them. But even as she approached the helicopter, she felt drawn to turn back.

"I'll stay here," she shouted to Brennan. "I'll make a shelter and wait for you. I'll keep watch." She couldn't abandon them. Not like this.

"We'll come back in the morning," Brenner shouted back, his voice nearly lost to the wind. He did not let go of her arm. "We'll come back, Ella. We'll bring them home!"

Reluctantly, she allowed herself to be led away. Once the storm cleared, and the sun came, she'd find answers.

Chapter 9

The morning sun arrived slowly, glimmering over the frozen wasteland, the silence so dense it was almost its own entity. The man clothed in wolf pelts lay prone, his body melding with mottled undergrowth, dusted above with snow. Nothing showed his presence, not even his breath, hidden by the muffler of skins over his nose and mouth. Only his eyes moved, gray as the ice along the frigid Alaskan coast. Through the scope of his high-caliber rifle, those eyes now fixed unblinking on a distant figure, lonely in the snow. The hunter's stillness held the electricity of intent.

His finger rested on the trigger, a conductor awaiting his moment. No. An executioner about to implement justice.

The fleeing figure darted across the white canvas, a shadow. It was a man this time, not the hunter's favorite, but it would do for today. The runner was trim if not youthful. He kept his body low as he pushed through the snow. He wore a long-sleeved black tee, a black wool hat that covered his hair (which the hunter knew was fluffy and corn-colored), gray corduroys and dark socks which from a distance might have been mistaken for boots if the snow here had been less than knee height.

"Any moment now..." The marksman watched as his quarry fell, floundering in the snow like a non-swimmer thrown in at the deep end of a pool. The hunter waited patiently, until his prey clambered back up and resumed his slog towards the sheltering trees, the same trees where his predator now waited.

The hunter's heartbeat synced with the rhythm of his quarry's flight, the tension winding tight around his chest. He adjusted the scope minutely—the crosshairs kissing the silhouette in the distance.

"Wait for it," an internal voice commanded, as clear as if his tongue hadn't been silenced by his own ruthless hand.

The moment stretched. The runner in the snow, heaving to breathe, made the mistake of straightening up to increase lung capacity. It was a fatal choice.

The hunter smiled as he pressed the trigger.

The shot pierced the stillness, an eruption that sent birds scattering from the scraggly pines. He watched, imagining the bullet traversing the open space, graceful and true, finding its mark. When his quarry threw up his hands at the collision of bullet into flesh, the hunter smiled again at this sign of his own artistry. Justice could be as magnificent as the Alaska mountains around them, jagged peaks reaching for the sky in triumph. Satisfaction surged through him like warm liquor.

"Beautiful," he mouthed soundlessly as his chest swelled with accomplishment.

He watched through the scope as the figure crumpled. This, too, brought him a visceral thrill, another testament to his skill. When he lowered his rifle, however, his face had again become an implacable mask, as if it were carved from the ice hanging from the mountain cliffs.

Silence reclaimed the frozen setting, and the scattered birds wheeled and returned to their homes. The man cradled his rifle, his breath an abominable whisper in the chill air. His companions crept forward from the tree line, their eyes aglow.

"Ha! Did you see that?" one murmured, shaking his head with an admiring grin. "The Wolf strikes true as ever."

"Like the hand of God himself," another added, a chuckle vibrating through his beard, frost clinging to the hairs like tiny crystals.

The man known as The Wolf did not share in their amusement. He simply stood there, acknowledging their admiration with the barest nod. His muteness was his own choice—a silence born of penitence and pain.

With an ease belying his bulk, he began to reload, his movements sure and silent. Three left-hand fingers—two missing, the stumps reminders of the day he'd enforced his own savage justice upon himself. One who dispensed justice, he believed, could not exclude himself. Those who knew the tale never discussed it with him; those who did not, understood not to ask.

In his mind, where vibrant dreams had once thrived, now he had only purpose and expiation. 'This is my atonement,' he thought, a silent internal litany. 'For each word I should not have spoken, for each action I cannot undo.'

"Look at him," one of the men said, his voice vibrating with fear and fascination. "Not a word, not a damn sound. It's like he's more beast than man."

"Shh," hissed Beardie, casting a wary glance at The Wolf. "He hears more than we say."

It was true. Every rustle of leaf, every murmur of wind, The Wolf heard—and understood. He no longer had spoken words to wield, but he had become fluent in the language of nature, in the secrets it revealed.

His granite gaze again contemplated the fallen figure in the distance, a dark splotch in the snow. To his audience, he seemed almost a creature of myth, an inscrutable god controlling the passage from life to death. As he moved to retrieve his newest tribute, he measured every step, wasting no energy on inessentials. Towering above the other hunters, his broad shoulders were draped in the thick pelts of wolves, the gray-white fur matted with flecks of crimson from prior conquests, like rubies on a monarch's cloak.

'Each piece I take,' he reflected, his inner voice as sharp as the knife he would soon draw, 'is a piece of myself I give away. A fair trade for my silence.'

"Never seen a man that size move so quiet," one of the men whispered. "Like he's part of the damn forest."

"Only quieter," another agreed, "Even real wolves yip and howl."

The Wolf pulled down his muffler, now that he had no need to conceal his presence. Lines of violence etched his face, including a jagged scar that ran like a dry riverbed across his cheek, and the line where his lips met, forever sealed by his own brutal handiwork.

The cold must have gnawed at his exposed flesh, but The Wolf seemed impervious to its bite. Snowflakes danced in the air, yet none seemed to settle on him, keeping their distance. Icicles, hanging from some of the higher tree branches, refracted his gray reflection. His long shadow and deep boot tracks tainted the pure snow, while his misting breath did the same to the air.

When the Wolf reached his fallen target, he knelt beside it, his mass blocking the view from his companions. The dead man lay twisted, arms outflung, and head turned to the side so that the bullet's entry hole was hidden from view. The still face expressed surprise, as though the man died wondering what he had done to deserve such an end. Well, the Wolf was not about to tell him. The body was cooling quickly, snow already providing a thin shroud. It was time for the holy moment.

The Wolf's hands, even lacking two fingers, worked delicately as he turned the corpse's head and opened its mouth. He pulled a knife from under his robes and held it up for all to see. Even in the weak winter light, its sharp edges flashed. The men across the clearing held their breath, their anticipation a palpable thing that seemed to swirl with the snowflakes in the air. The Wolf's arm thrust down the knife.

Finally, The Wolf's hand emerged, crimson-stained and clutching his prize—a human tooth. The sight of it sent a shiver through the onlookers, not from the cold, but from what it represented.

"Damn," someone muttered. "He got it."

There was no smile on The Wolf's face, no triumphant gleam in his eye—only the stillness of a predator who claimed his due. He rose to full height, still holding the grim token aloft. The other men's reactions varied from approving nods to swallowed gasps. It was a ritual enacted many times before, yet never losing its potency.

"Bravo," one man dared to break the silence, clapping slowly, the sound crisp and solitary.

In response, The Wolf merely bowed his head. He had no words to offer. His language was one of action and consequence, spoken through the precision of his aim and the finality of his blade. He held the tooth like an offering in the upright palm of his bloody hand as he moved back towards the waiting figures.

"Ever think he regrets it?" The quiet question came from the youngest among them.

"Regrets what? Being the best damn hunter this side of the mountains?" scoffed one of the others.

"Cutting out his own tongue... his fingers..." The younger man shuddered.

"Boy, we've all done things—things that haunt us. Things that change us." The older guy shrugged. "But he's turned his tragedy into excellence. And he gets rid of vermin. Helps the rest of us."

The Wolf felt their stares but ignored them. He knew they were too awed and unskilled to do anything that might hurt him in any real way. Instead, he lifted a small screwdriver from his hunting belt. Scraping with the tool, he began whittling through the tooth's enamel, with slow, meticulous motions. His companions watched, not speaking.

Finally, once he'd bored the thin hole, he pulled the clasp at his neck and withdrew his necklace. The makeshift beads clacked as he held the necklace up. Teeth swayed about. More than he could count. He slipped the newest prize onto the end, and then turned, striding away.

His entourage followed, clumsy in the drifts, their own rifles shouldered as they chased the man in the wolf pelts. This was just the first round. There was more hunting planned for the day.

Chapter 10

Ella Porter stood at the edge of the clearing, her breath visible in the chilly dawn. Even though the sun hadn't fully risen, it was nearly ten o'clock. A night shrieking with winds and snow, had now yielded too bright, almost blinding, sunshine sparkling off the drifts on the grounds and the clumps decorating the black spruce. She could still see a couple of clouds crossed beyond the mountains, taking the storm further inland.

"Nature's own drama," she muttered to herself, pulling her jacket closer against the residual chill. The storm had scrubbed the sky to a rare porcelain blue, another sign of nature celebrating.

She turned away from the horizon, scanning the landscape, seeing past the magnificence, knowing grimness awaited.

A biting chill hung in the air as she made her way through the new drifts in the clearing that she and Brenner had left just hours before. Ahead, an errant flap of blue marked the ground where they had made their gruesome discovery. Now, the bodies lay partly covered, the snow adding a lacey veil of modesty over the women's place of abandonment.

She murmured, her voice barely above a whisper, "It's like they're sleeping."

Ella knelt beside the first corpse. She studied the woman's face. The blonde hair splayed out on the snow reminded Ella of her own, and for a moment, her twin sister Priscilla's face flashed in her mind—an image of scorn and estrangement.

"Any I.D.?" called Brenner from behind her.

"Nothing yet." Ella returned her attention to the woman in the snow, taking in the fair complexion, and the frost clinging to the fine hairs along the woman's cheek—like dew on gossamer webs. The features were intact – aquiline nose with a diamond stud through a nostril piercing, slight nicotine yellowing on the cheeks, triple-pierced ears with golden skulls hanging from the rings. The upper tips of her ears, exposed to the elements by her short coiffure, had darkened with frostbite. A slight trace of blood stained her thin lips. Whoever had killed her had no desire to fully obliterate her identity.

Ella hunkered down next to the second figure. This woman's dark coarse hair fanned out from beneath her head like an ink blot against the white snow. Her olive skin had a ghastly pallor in death, but it was her strong jawline that set her apart. Even in death, she looked like someone who did not brook disrespect.

Her mouth was mostly open, as though ready to scold a miscreant. The lips were coated with blood spatter, but the cause was evident.

"Look at this," Ella pulled back the woman's shirt collar to completely reveal a deep gash across her throat. The blood on the edges had hardened to scarlet frost. "No hesitation." There was something surgical about the wound—precise and confident.

"Professional hit, or personal vendetta?" Brenner's voice was a low rumble over her shoulder.

"Could be either," Ella replied, her mind toggling between profiles and motives, "but there's anger here. This wasn't quick."

She noted a tapestry of bruises along the woman's arms. "She fought back hard," Ella felt a swell of respect rising amidst the horror. "It's like they shot her with an arrow, then finished the kill with a knife in an extra measure of brutality."

"Like a doe in the field."

Ella touched the ruined shirt collar again. "Who were you?" she whispered. It was a question she asked every victim, a silent vow to give them back their names, to restore the identities stolen by violence. She let out a slow breath, the weight of sorrow pressing against her professional detachment for a moment.

At last she stood up and moved to the third body, her heart even heavier, because this was Kerry's friend, the woman who had tried to give her a new life away from fear and abuse.

The red-haired woman – Emma - lay with an unnatural stillness, her freckled skin dotted with ice crystals as if she were a figure in some grotesque fairy tale. A slender build made her appear almost childlike, a vulnerability that tugged at Ella's heartstrings.

"Red hair... Freckles... " Ella began, her voice trailing off as she took in the uniqueness of this last victim. "A girl next-door appeal. Doesn't look like the others in that sense. Even Kerry has signs of hard living."

"Every detail could be a piece of the puzzle," Brenner reminded her, watching as she inspected the corpse.

"Exactly. Or maybe she just got in the way, as Kerry implied." Ella's eyes locked onto a peculiar, crescent-shaped scar near the woman's collarbone—a distinctive mark that would have been hidden under most necklines. "This scar—it's old. Healed well. I take back what I said about no hard living. It looks like an old knife wound."

Brenner squatted down to get a better look, extending his left leg to keep the pressure off. "Maybe that's why she took Kerry in without question. She had once known what it was to be afraid of someone in her life." He took several pictures with his phone.

“Maybe so.” Ella went back to studying the scene, her brain cataloging the information she saw. Except for the shirt collar, she had not touched anything. She did not want to disturb the crime scene. Even so, the evidence of her eyes had her thoughts spinning, twisting details into a thread of narrative. Three women with lives cruelly ended, and a fourth who lived in fear, yet the story was incomplete.

"Let's get these photos to HQ, see if we can make any matches," Brenner suggested.

Ella stood back, absorbing the scene from a distance. The three women seemed almost like discarded dolls in a child's playroom, their lives reduced to props in a macabre set piece. She circled them, cataloging their final poses.

The first woman, her blonde hair dusted with snow, lay splayed with her arms reaching out as if she had tried to fend off her fate. Ella noted the rips in her clothing—fabric that was once perhaps a warm embroidered coat now hung in tatters, revealing glimpses of skin marred with bruises and dirt. Patches of dried blood clung to the wool like dark, sinister blossoms.

"Look at this," Ella said, pointing to the jagged tear across the hem of the woman's shirt. "She struggled too. There was a fight."

Brenner nodded, his eyes scanning for details that might have escaped hers. "Defensive wounds," he murmured, indicating where the fabric bunched around the wrists.

The second woman's attire was no less battered; her shirt, half-torn from her arms, fluttered lightly in the frigid breeze, while her pants were smeared with mud and something darker.

"God, what did they go through?" Tears pricked at the back of her eyelids, but she blinked them away.

"Too much."

They returned to the third victim. Her red hair stood out like a halo against the white blanket of snow. Her clothing was in rags; her silver silk blouse hung off one shoulder, stained with scarlet. Her bare feet bore the bruised splotches of advancing frostbite, as did several of her fingertips.

Only now, after studying each woman to get a feel for whom they were, did Ella consider the arrows that had ended their lives, still protruding from their chests. "These arrows...they're not just off the shelf, are they?" she asked, turning to Brenner. "They look specialized, handmade maybe?"

"Could be," Brenner acknowledged, his fingers hovering inches from the wooden shaft of the closest arrow, careful not to touch. "Not your typical sporting goods store stock."

Ella watched him, his sniper's eyes assessing the angle and penetration—a professional's appraisal of a colleague's deadly handiwork. When he stood up, he gestured to the arrow in Emma's neck, right where throat met collarbone. "This one looks like it was shot from close range. Look how deep it is, the shaft barely visible. Whoever the hunter is, Miles Cruise or someone else, he killed the other two women from a distance. He's quite a talented shot."

Ella blew out a breath and watched it condense in the air. "Handmade arrows could mean traceable arrows," she thought aloud. "They look unique enough to lead us somewhere."

"Or to someone." Brenner crouched again beside the first corpse, his shadow falling over the arrow. "Look at this fletching," he said.

Ella knelt beside him, her eyes tracing the carved feathers of the arrows. The vane was cut from actual feathers, each barb delicately trimmed and adhered in a fashion that was both archaic and artistic. It was a stark contrast to the brutality of their use.

"See how evenly the feathers are spaced?" Brenner continued, his large hands deftly rotating around the arrow to frame it. "That takes a steady hand. Someone made these with a lot of care. That takes meticulous craftsmanship."

"Which suggests they're more than just weapons," Ella added in. "Whoever made them sees them as works of art." She reached out but stopped short of touching, respecting the sanctity of the crime scene. The wood of the shaft was polished to a shine, reflecting sunlight along the grain. "Someone took a lot of time over this."

"Whoever did this wanted to leave their mark," Brenner agreed, his gaze lingering on the arrow. "Custom-made," he concluded. "Hand-made. Each arrow is probably unique."

"Which means they might lead back to our killer," Ella said, pulling herself up to stand, impelled by the excitement of the possibility. "If we can find where they came from, we might find who's responsible for this." Her eyes shone with animation. They were getting somewhere. She remembered the guilt that had sunk her spirits during the night when she had had to leave the women alone in the dark. Now daylight had uncovered some clues. She would be able to move ahead with this information to do right by the women in every successive step of the investigation.

"Exactly," Brenner rose to join her. His eyes rested on her, drinking in her newfound confidence.

"Let's get these documented properly," Ella decided, reaching for her camera. "Every detail could be key."

Even as she moved around again, snapping photos, she became aware of a distant buzz floating towards them on the wind. After a minute or two, she identified it as the rhythmic chopping of helicopter blades. Ella tilted her head, listening as the sound grew steadily louder. The sun glinted off her blonde ponytail and the reflectors at the cuffs of her dark blue FBI parka. She didn't need to see the choppers to know what was coming—the crime scene processors were on their way.

"Finally," she exhaled, putting hands to waist and bending back to stretch her spine after crouching so much. Things were beginning to move more quickly. Her fingers instinctively brushed against the badge clipped to her belt, a reminder of the responsibility she carried. The forensics team would depend on her local knowledge, and she was determined not to let them—or the victims—down.

The approaching helicopters roared into the valley. Birds took flight en-masse; a fox raced under the low pine branches into the sparse woods beyond. "So much for quiet mornings in Nome," Ella murmured, half-smiling.

Then she looked at the bodies at her feet again, and the chuckle died away. She squared her shoulders as she watched the mechanical birds advance and circle the clearing, a carrion above the corpses. The snowstorm might have passed, but another tempest was just beginning, and Ella Porter was at its center.

The helicopters descended with imperial authority, churning up a blizzard of snowflakes in their wake, perhaps in retribution for the battering winds of the night before. The first touched down about fifty yards from Ella, its skids compressing the new snow. The second landed nearer to where Ella and Brenner's own chopper had touched down, its pilot setting the runners across some elk tracks. Almost immediately, both choppers began to disgorge their passengers, all of them in warm bulky jackets, and many in snow or ski pants.

"Watch your backs!" Ella called out to the local officers securing the perimeter. Her voice was firm, but she couldn't mask a tremor of excitement. This was what she trained for—what drove her back to Nome despite the shadows it cast on her past.

She approached the now stationary machines, their rotors coughing to a stop.

"Agent Porter, FBI," she introduced herself briskly to the disembarking personnel. "I'll be your point of contact here."

"Let's hope you can shed some light on this mess," replied the lead forensics agent, taking the case passed out to him by another agent still in the vehicle. He turned to Ella, nodding an afterthought greeting. "Which way is the scene?"

"That way about fifty yards," Ella didn't take his brusqueness personally. She too wanted to get on with it.

Around her, nature seemed to hold its breath—the tall pines standing sentinel, the vast Alaskan sky stretched clear and blue. On the ground, however, activity bustled. The forensics team fanned out, everyone to their particular areas, snapping on latex gloves and readying their evidence collection gear. They cast long, midday shadows that doubled their number and accompanied them across the landscape.

She spotted a small, scruffy looking man emerging from the far chopper, using Brenner's shoulder for balance: Dr. Simmons, the coroner.

He had donned a white lab coat over his parka, to make sure everyone could recognize and find him. He was slender, but with so many layers of clothes he looked like a snow clown plodding into a circus ring. His lab coat flapped against the top of his boots and dragged in the higher drifts as he maneuvered awkwardly toward the crime scene. His gray eyes and hair looked wild with indignation. Ella could see the exhaustion etched in the deep lines on his forehead, evidence of the countless autopsies he had performed in his career. But beneath that weariness, she detected a glimmer of eagerness. Like her, he loved a puzzle.

Ella headed in his direction, sure footed despite being shorter than he was. In response, he scowled at her. She remained unbothered. Dr. Simmons was known for his unorthodox methods and unconventional attire, but his expertise and sharp mind were second to none. She had worked with him on previous cases, and there was a mutual respect that had formed between them despite their differences.

"Dr. Simmons, good to have you here," Ella greeted, extending her hand for a firm shake.

Simmons' spectacles had fogged in the cold, and now he took them off to polish them. Once back on, the coroner scanned the scene, taking in every detail just as Ella had when she first arrived. His grizzled beard twitched as he replied. "Agent Porter, you've brought me quite a puzzle this time." His voice was as gravelly as the grit on Nome's streets.

"A nasty one. Three women, all killed with arrows, one of them mutilated after death. The arrows are custom-made," Ella summarized, gesturing towards the victims. "It seems like there's plenty more to uncover."

A tired smile tugged at the corners of his mouth. "I'll do my best, Agent Porter. I hear you've been here twice already."

Ella nodded, her gaze drifting back to the crime scene where Brenner was now conferring with one of the forensic photographers. The peculiar arrows still protruded from the victims like macabre ornaments. She and the doctor began to walk in tandem toward the crime scene, now bound by yellow police tape, an odd sight in the wilderness.

"We landed for a few minutes during the night, then the storm got too much. We – Brenner and I – got here as soon as we could this morning. I'm glad the rest of you are here now. We need all hands on deck."

"Although your sense of duty is commendable, Agent Porter, I hope you haven't been messing up my crime scene with all your tromping around." With those words, Dr. Simmons adjusted his glasses and stepped closer to examine the bodies, shivering slightly as a gust of wind swept through the clearing.

She watched as he approached the blue tarp, cursing and stumbling. He was excellent in the lab; not so much in the snow.

The coroner knelt beside the first of the victims, the blonde. An assistant followed, offering material and bags as needed. The silence around Simmons was punctuated only by the soft clicking of a camera and the murmur of the wind through the trees.

"Notice anything peculiar about the clothing?" Dr. Simmons asked aloud, not really expecting anyone to answer.

"Torn and ripped."

"Not that," he said, impatiently. "I mean the style. Look."

She did, and now she noticed what he meant. Ella stepped closer to see better, her eyes narrowing. "They're not from here," she observed. "The fabric, the cut... it doesn't match what most people in Nome wear."

"Indeed," the coroner nodded, a teacher pleased with a pupil's response. "And look at the stitching on the plaquettes and the cuffs. It's custom, but it's not standard Western European or American designers. And the patterns certainly aren't Asian or African. These garments suggest Eastern European origins, I think."

Ella's heart skipped a beat. Immigrants? Or something more nefarious? Her mind raced with the implications. Had they been brought here against their will? Smuggling, human trafficking—the possibilities were dark and numerous.

"Let's see if we can ID them," Dr. Simmons continued, moving on to examine the hands of the victims. He sighed when he picked up Emma's hand, with its blue-black beginnings of necrosis, and laid it down tenderly before nodding at a forensic technician to begin work.

Silence fell as the group watched the technician run a portable fingerprint scanner over the lifeless fingers of each victim. Ella herself followed every motion, every attempt to coax the machine into yielding information that identified the women there.

"Nothing," the technician finally announced, his voice laced with frustration. "No matches in any database we have access to."

"Nothing at all?" Brenner Gunn voiced the astonishment of all of them.

"Not a single one," confirmed Dr. Simmons, standing up. He peered at Ella, and the strong lenses of his glasses made his eyes look owlish. Owlish and surprised out of professional detachment. "It's as if they've never existed in any system we know."

Ella felt a shiver travel up her spine despite the sun beginning to warm the air around them. No identities, no history, no ties to anywhere. They had seemingly been plucked from obscurity, to meet their ends in this desolate place.

"I have something else," Dr. Simmons motioned for Ella and Brenner to come closer. The coroner stood next to the unknown brunette. Ignoring both the arrow and the slash to her throat, he directed their attention to her lips. "Do you see that blood?"

Brenner nodded.

Ella licked her lips, chapped from all the time in the winter air. "From her neck cut, yes?"

"Some, surely," the doctor agreed, "but not all. Look here." He had a small flashlight in hand, which he handed to Ella, as he pulled a laser pointer from a pocket in his lab coat. "Turn the flashlight on and shine it into her mouth."

When Ella did so, Simmons clicked on the laser pointer. He shone the red dot into the woman's illuminated mouth. "See that?"

The laser point rested on a new gap between the teeth in the woman's lower jaw, a tear in the gum where the first lower molar had rested. "That's a postmortem wound," he said. "See how it hardly bled? The poor woman's heart wasn't pumping anymore."

“Good God,” Brenner’s eyes mirrored the nausea roiling in Ella’s gut. “You mean—”

“Whoever killed them took a trophy. He took a tooth.” Simmons rose and went to the body of the blonde, used the back of the laser pointer to pull down her lip just a little. Another gap showed there. “He took a tooth from these two. I’ll need to get the other body back to the lab and let it thaw before I can get its mouth open, but I’m almost sure, from the blood at the corner of her mouth, that this woman was violated in the same way.”

“He keeps trophies,” Ella repeated. “He pulls out their teeth after they are dead.”

“Just so,” said Simmons. He stood and walked to the other end of the mass grave. They joined him. “Now,” he continued, “Look at their feet.”

Ella bent and reached out gingerly with her black-gloved hand, as though her touch could somehow reverberate back through time and offer warmth. The skin of each woman’s feet was marred by frostbite, blackened and raw. "They ran through the woods without shoes... in the middle of winter."

"Or were forced to," added Brenner, his own arms suddenly crossed tightly against the cold, as if he were reliving the women’s final hours.

Ella's gaze traced the cruel lines of frostbite ascending the limbs. Each toe seemed to speak of miles trekked, of unfathomable fear and pain. “Who would do this?" she whispered, not expecting an answer. She was used to crimes where greed, ambition, jealousy or possession motivated killers. This was something else. Something wilder than animals. Animals didn’t kill just for fun, for trophies.

"Agent Porter, take a look at this," one of the forensics analysts called out, gesturing her over to the two women lying side by side. As Ella approached, the analyst pointed to their arms. There, etched into the skin with ink that had long since faded to a murky blue, were tattoos. Identical markings that resembled some sort of crest or symbol—a bird in flight, encircled by thorny vines.

The tattoos looked old... at least a few years old judging by the fading. It was a unique enough tattoo, that it might help them ID the victims.

She took out her phone, snapping pictures of the emblem.

The bird in flight encircled by vines almost seemed poetic as she stared at it. These women had been ensnared as well... But where were the thorns?

She turned, searching the horizon, her eyes narrowed.

On one hand, the tattoos might help them ID the victims. The custom arrows might ID the killer. And the hunters they'd arrested the previous night, who'd had the woman in the cage, might lead them to Miles Cruise.

She couldn't stay here any longer. Forensics would bring the women's bodies back to civilization. Her job now was to find out who they were. Equally important, her job was to find out who had done this, and end their spree, make sure they were stopped.

She turned to Brenner, letting Simmons and the forensic team get on with their work. "Want to linger here or head back and speak to the assholes from last night, see what they know about all this?"

Brenner's jaw tightened. "Let's head back," he replied. "We need to squeeze every ounce of information out of those bastards."

Ella nodded. They needed every clue they could get. Her mind flitted to Miles Cruise. Did the FBI know what he'd been involved in? Was that why she'd been assigned to this?

Something felt off, but she couldn't say what... They needed to find Cruise. If anyone had answers about the victims and their mysterious tattoos, it was him.

Ella turned, tramping towards the waiting helicopter. In her hand, she clutched her phone, the pictures of the tattoos and arrows already sent for examination.

Her other hand clenched tightly.

The hunters had caged a woman... And now they were the ones behind bars.

It was time to see how much they liked this change of roles.

Chapter 11

Ella marched into the interrogation room and slapped her file down on the table at its center.

She looked around, approving what she saw. The room was small, about 8 x 10. A gray metal table with a scarred oak top took up the center of the space. It looked like something ejected from a school science lab forty years ago. A pair of metal chairs sat facing each other across the table. Ella knew that both chairs on the interviewee side had uneven legs and tilted slightly forward. Anyone who sat there would constantly have to work against gravity to stay in place. Adding to their discomfort, the chairs sat right below the heating vent in the ceiling. Zoned heating at the station meant the interrogation room temperature could be whatever the officers wanted. Ella happened to know that the heat was off, and the air conditioning on, which is why she wore a chunky navy sweater monogrammed with three huge letters in yellow: FBI. To add to the ambience, the color scheme in the room was mildew brown below and slime green above the dingy chair rail.

It was the perfect room in which to interview a contemptible crook.

She studied the man at the table.

He was one of the hunters she had caught and cuffed the previous night. He had started that evening's adventure in chic gear and a sense of privilege. Today, after a night in the cells, he looked almost like what he aspired to be: a rugged, unkempt hunter with the spirit of the untamed Alaskan wilderness. His hair was a tousled mess of dark waves, strewn with flecks of gray and the debris of tundra brush. Stubble lined his jaw and his eyes were gritty with sleeplessness.

He had shed his coat on intake, and now wore only a camo t-shirt and trousers, each crumpled and stained from his flight to escape and from sharing his cell with less fastidious roommates. Mud still caked his boots. His breath was foul.

It was clear that he had not accepted his situation, however. He crossed his legs as though leading a board meeting, hands folded on the table. "I've got nothing to say to you until my lawyer arrives." He smiled smugly, leaning back in his chair. The action tilted his chair to the left and he slid from his posture of power, hastily uncrossing his legs to brace them on the floor.

Ella hid a twinkle and circled back to her own chair, pulling it from the table. The metal legs scraped on the floor, like fingernails on a blackboard. The would-be poacher winced. She settled into her chair, relaxed and at ease. She did not smile.

She knew his name was Tyrone Kogan, and he was Chief Financial Officer of an investment company in San Francisco, with a previous conviction for tax fraud.

Brenner leaned against the wall behind her, the one with the two-way window. He'd been pacing like a caged tiger, back and forth, back and forth, not because he was nervous, but as another way of aggravating the witness. She knew the pacing would begin again when Brenner thought the time was right.

The air conditioning kicked on. The cold air blew straight down on the poacher. He flinched again. "Hey! What's with the cold air?"

"It's winter in Alaska," Ella said calmly. "It gets cold."

She locked eyes with the hunter, blue meeting murky green.

"Turn off the fan," he ordered. "I'm cold."

"I'm not cold," Ella patted the cuffs of her wool sweater. "Brenner, are you cold?"

"Not at all. Quite comfortable. And the fan's on a timer, by the way," he addressed the poacher, "it just does its thing."

The hunter shifted in his seat, sullen and trying not to shiver. Ella leaned forward and put her badge on the table, where it glinted under the sterile light.

"Look, we can do this the easy way or the hard way," she said, conversationally. "Yesterday you made a really dumb mistake, running away from officers. But I'm not your enemy. What I really need is answers."

"Answers..." Tyrone Kogan's voice trailed off. Ella could see goose bumps on the back of his wrists where his cuffs rucked up a bit. He said nothing else, just shrugged.

Of the three men they'd managed to bring back in cuffs, he was the only one cleared by doctors for interrogation. Two others had frostbitten feet. The fourth was in critical condition.

Brenner Gunn resumed pacing, his shadow accompanying him. He barely bothered to look at the man in the chair. Ella knew Brenner well enough to realize for him, Tyrone Kogan was beneath contempt. He'd been part of a gang that had a woman trapped in a cage, and for Brenner, that made Kogan lower than a cockroach.

"Let's talk about the woman," Ella began, her tone measured, eyes locked on his face. "The one in the cage in your Jeep."

His gaze remained fixed on a nondescript point on the table, features set in hard lines. Not a muscle twitched, not an eyebrow raised; he was a study in stoicism.

"Did you think it was normal?" she pressed, leaning forward slightly. "To lock a human being up in a cage?"

He shrugged. "It wasn't my Jeep. I was just along for the ride. Maybe she liked it. How would I know? Besides, who are you to talk?" He almost spat the words. "You had *me* locked up in a cage last night and this morning."

Ella exhaled slowly and slid a photograph across the table toward him. It showed the metal cage sitting in the ice along the highway, grim against the backdrop of the rugged terrain.

"Look at this," she insisted. "Doesn't this stir anything in you?"

He glanced at the picture, shrugged again. There was no flicker of remorse or defiance in his eyes, just indignation that he had to face consequences for his actions.

As she watched him, Ella sifted every piece of evidence, every scrap of testimony they had collected. She thought of Kerry Lonigan, of the hopelessness that had nearly crushed her. Kerry's life might be blighted, and this toad offered only obstinate silence.

"Doesn't it bother you?" Her question was an arrow aimed at his conscience. "That could've been someone you know, someone you care about."

"But it wasn't. So—Not my problem."

He didn't care at all. At these words, Ella wanted to snatch up the chair next to her and crash it down over his head. Cilla would have done it.

But she wasn't Cilla. She did not want to be Cilla. So she drew in a breath that stung her lungs with the cold, sterile air of the interrogation room and pushed a photo of Kerry in the cage across the table.

"Mr. Kogan, it actually is your problem. You see, you're facing charges of aiding and abetting a kidnapping. This woman," she tapped the image, "was found in a cage, in a car with you. A car in which you spent an evening travelling, sitting right in front of her."

Kogan sat a little straighter now. But the glance he gave the photo skittered away like a stone over ice.

"Kidnapping's not my style," he said superciliously. "You can't pin that on me."

"No? Then what about murder?" Ella laid down two more photographs. One showed the bodies of the three women in the snow, the central focus on the distinctive arrows embedded in their chests. The other was a closeup of the still unidentified brunette with the gash at her throat. "Murder, Mr. Kogan. Is that serious enough to concern you?" Her finger paused on each face, the faces of women who would never again feel the crisp air of Nome or any other place.

His recoil was immediate. The chair rocked and almost tipped over, he shoved it back so forcefully. His veneer of arrogance slipped, his features seeming to melt into panic. His hand trembled before he clenched it into a fist. "I haven't killed anyone," he insisted, his voice ragged. "I had nothing to do with *that*."

"Explain," Ella's gaze locked onto his. She studied the hunter, looking for the fissures in his rugged facade.

Kogan pushed his chair further back from the table, only to find himself stopped because Brenner was behind him.

"Stay in your seat, Kogan." Brenner did not bother to hide his scorn. "We aren't done yet."

"Murder is a serious charge, Mr. Kogan. Three women, their lives snuffed out. You need to start talking, or—" Ella paused, letting the threat hang in the chilled air.

"Look, I'm a hunter, sort of, but game, not... not people." He swallowed hard, his Adam's apple bobbing like a buoy at sea. "I didn't kill anyone. You gotta believe me."

"Belief has nothing to do with it. Someone killed them. Someone who goes on illegal hunts. And we have evidence here—" she tapped her folder, "—that you've gone on similar hunts. So here you are, with evidence stacking up against you."

"But I haven't done anything!"

"Let's pretend, just for the moment, that I do believe you." Ella's tone made clear that this was merely hypothetical. "What kind of hunter are you, "sort of?"

The hunter's hands were clenched so tightly that his knuckles blanched, the veins on his well-manicured hands bulging painfully. "I've done nothing," he repeated, but there was a tremor in his voice now.

Ella straightened her spine as she leaned hard against the table, invading the space that separated her from the Kogan. Now she could feel the cold downdraft directly. It focused her senses like a whetstone on a blade.

"Let's talk about your hobbies," Ella taunted, "the hunting group you were so eager to join. Must've sounded like quite the party. We saw you join them back at the bar. Then the Jeep with the caged woman picked you up." At this, he lowered his gaze, avoiding hers.

Kogan grunted, his gaze fixed on a scratch on the battered table. His hands, now unclenched, fidgeted with the hem of his camouflage shirt.

"Who introduced you to this exclusive club?" she pressed on, tilting her head slightly, mocking him. "You strike me as a man who doesn't find pleasure in the usual pastimes. So, what was it? The thrill? The camaraderie?"

"It was just about hunting, hunting without rules, while we got the hang of it. Hunting animals with tracking devices, so we could find them more easily." He looked a little embarrassed at having to admit he had to cheat to get a shot. Then he perked up. "But we hunted in the dark to give them a chance, so that wasn't so bad. It evened the odds, you might say."

Ella let that sink in for a minute, fitting that with the evidence of the bodies on the tundra. Her hand itched to grab that chair again, but again she stayed her impulse. She decided to change the subject and maybe circle back. "Who was your buddy? The one we arrested with you?"

He stiffened in his chair and raised an arrogant chin. "None of those men were my buddies. I've got better taste than that."

"So how'd you hear about the hunting group? That bar?"

"Just heard."

"Someone brought you in," Ella insisted, her mind weaving through the information, trying to connect unseen dots. "Someone you're protecting. Why?"

"Look, my girl," Kogan flashed, "I'm saying nothing more. I signed a non-disclosure agreement and I'm a businessman of ethics."

"A man of ethics with a fraud conviction, participating in illegal poaching? I don't think so. I think you're afraid." Ella watched as the hunter's Adam's apple bobbed again, the muscles in his neck tensing as if preparing for a blow.

Inside, Ella felt frustration and revulsion gnawing at the edges of her professional calm. Brenner was right—she hated when women were harmed, but her anger was a controlled burn, fueling pursuit of justice. She knew the man across from her was not a mastermind, but she also knew he held information that frightened him. And his lawyer would be landing in Nome within a couple of hours.

"Okay, let's try another approach," Ella suggested, her voice softer now, almost persuasive. "Help us understand why you didn't leave when you realized what was going on. Help yourself."

The hunter's lips parted, then pressed closed. "Lawyer," was all he said.

Ella glanced over her shoulder at Brenner, whose pacing had ceased. His night-blue eyes reflected both concern and a hint of admiration for her relentless questioning. She wanted to be back on the chase, but if she pushed too hard now, the lawyer could shred any case she developed from Kogan's words.

And then Kogan himself reopened the door a crack. "Besides," he added. "That girl? The one you found. I didn't know. Didn't know she was going to be there."

He'd chosen to continue speaking. A gray area.

Ella leaned forward, the metal chair's edge digging into her thighs, a physical echo of her incredulity. "You're saying you didn't see her? That girl, locked up like an animal?" She tossed the photograph back onto the table, its edges fluttering before it landed with the image facing him—the girl, eyes wide as Arctic moons.

"No," Kogan grumbled. He refused to look at the photo. "I'm saying I didn't know she was going to be there. All I knew was that we were going to hunt some illegal game, put one over on the state and the feds."

"Let me get this straight," Ella said, her tone measured, but insistent. "You're out there with a group that's hunting illegally, and you expect me to believe you didn't notice a human being trapped in a cage?"

"Of course I noticed," he said irritably, and the chair rocked again. "But not until I was in the car. And then it was too late to change my mind."

Ella pressed, knowing she had to keep him talking, keep peeling back the layers of his story. "Why didn't you leave when you realized what was happening?"

His jaw clenched visibly. "I was scared, alright? I knew they were poachers. I knew they were bad news. That was the thrill. But if I left before the hunt even began . . . "

"Scared?" Ella echoed, seizing on the crack in his rugged facade. She noted Brenner's stance stiffen; they both recognized the shift in the hunter's demeanor. "So, you went along because you were afraid? You, the mighty adventurer?"

"Yes, I was afraid! You don't just walk away from a crowd like that. Do it and they'll hunt you. But I didn't *know* they liked to hunt people until I got in that car, and then it was too late. My skin was on the line. I've got a company relying on me, business deals, a slew of employees. It was that girl or my life and mine was more important."

Ella studied him, searching his face for any sign of deceit. Kogan looked back at her, his own gaze almost pleading. "And the murders?" she asked softly.

"I didn't kill anybody," he stated flatly. "Why do you think I ran away when I had the chance? I didn't want to pay for their crimes."

"Yet, here we are," Ella said, leaning back in her chair, the photograph of the girl in the cage a silent witness to the hunter's statement. She let the implication hang in the air, as chilling as the draught blowing down from the ceiling. "What about Miles Cruise?"

The name fell into the room like a lead weight, and Kogan looked away, his face losing color.

"N-never heard of him," he stammered.

Ella felt a surge of adrenaline. The mention of the poacher struck a nerve.

"Come on," Ella pressed, her voice a mix of sympathy and steel. "Miles Cruise is no ghost story around these parts."

"Look, I—" He choked back the words and compressed his lips.

"Talk to me," Ella urged, her own heart pounding. They were getting closer to something, she knew it. "What did Miles do to make you this scared?"

Silence stretched taut between them, the only sound Brenner's uneven footsteps as he paced behind her, the tap of his boot against the concrete floor a metronome counting out Kogan's rising tension.

The hunter glanced at Brenner, then at Ella. He looked almost yearning, ready to snatch at a sense of safety. Then the light in his eyes died.

"I want my lawyer," he repeated. "I won't talk again without my lawyer."

Ella sat back, her mind racing. This was it—the wall they'd hit time and time again. She glanced at Brenner, whose jaw tightened, the muscle ticking in frustration. They both knew what the hunter's demand meant: silence now, maybe forever. Their window into the twisted world of poachers and their prey was closing again.

"Alright," Ella conceded with a nod, even as dread settled in her gut. "We can wait."

Brenner knocked on the door, and two marshals entered the room. They approached the suspect, and each took an arm. Kogan got up, his shoulders hunched, and slunk from the room.

Ella and Brenner exchanged a look. They had names, suspicions, but the path to the truth remained hidden in a thick fog of fear and silence.

"Damn it," Brenner muttered, his limp more pronounced as he turned to lean against the wall. "We are so close."

"Close doesn't solve cases." She gathered the pictures and put them back in the file, slapped the file on the table in frustration. They needed Miles Cruise. Miles Cruise was the thread that would lead them out of this labyrinth.

Ella Porter stared at the spot where the hunter had been seated moments before. She envisioned his terrified expression when she'd uttered Miles Cruise's name.

"Poachers," Brenner said, breaking the quiet. He leaned against the wall, arms crossed over his chest. "They're a cowardly breed. But fear... fear can make a man sing."

"Or shut him up tight." Ella got up and walked to the interrogation window. Her breath fogged up the glass, and she drew an absentminded circle with her finger.

"Did you see his eyes, Brenner?" Her voice was barely above a whisper. "When I mentioned Cruise, it was as if he saw a ghost."

"Maybe he did," Brenner straightened from the wall, began to pace again. Moving kept his thoughts going. "Figuratively speaking. Everyone around here knows the rumors about Cruise. If half of what they say is true..."

Ella turned back to look at him, her eyes searching his for certainty. "We need to find out the rest—about Cruise, the hunters, everything."

Brenner nodded, but there was a crease of worry between his brows. "It's going to be harder now that he's lawyered up. We've lost momentum."

"Then we'll just have to push harder," Ella stated, more confidently than she felt.

"How?" insisted Brenner.

"Cruise. The key is Cruise. I want to dig a bit deeper. See exactly who he is."

Chapter 12

Ella Porter leaned against the break room counter, her fingers drumming a staccato rhythm on the faux marble surface. With each tap, her eyes flicked toward the door, willing it to open and bring news of an expelled attorney from their midst.

But for now, their suspect was still engaged with legal counsel.

And it wasn't like she thought he was the organizer behind all of this anyway. No... no, that credit went to Miles Cruise.

Beside her, Brenner Gunn stood rigid, his lips pressed into a line of frustration that pulled at the scar on his cheek. He stretched his hands—once weapons of precision, now stymied from action.

"Any minute now," Ella muttered, tapping faster.

"Minute feels like an hour today," Brenner agreed, his deep voice exasperated. He glanced down and pulled his sleeve back to reveal his wristwatch. The action also revealed the puckering of another scar, one that snaked up his arm—an unwanted tattoo of his past.

"Tick, tock..." Ella grumbled, her gaze locked on the screen of her laptop sitting on the counter. A buffering bar loitered there. It had been clogging up her screen for over fifteen minutes.

Finally, the file loaded.

"Shit, who knew AI would be this slow?" Brenner remarked. "I thought it was supposed to speed things up. Tell me again what this shit is?"

"It's a modular package for facial recognition," Ella explained. "It plugs into AI generated images and compares the database with the photo we feed it."

"So... what's in the database?"

"The internet," she said simply. "The AI scours the internet for faces. Anywhere. Everywhere. Not just faces, but any distinguishing mark."

"The computer can recognize that?"

She nodded. "Alright. Package is loaded."

The flicker of the computer screen cast an eerie glow over Ella's eyes, giving them a greenish cast. Her gaze narrowed as she analyzed the cascading lines of code and surveillance images that flooded the AI program's interface. She hunched forward slightly, a lock of blonde hair flopping over her forehead. She was so absorbed, she left it untouched. Her fingers danced over the keyboard, commanding the software to cull global databases for Miles Cruise's visage.

"Come on," she urged under her breath, "show up you slippery bastard."

Because the word command hadn't worked, she now plugged in an image Miles Cruise. A clean cut, scowling face. A man who looked like a banker in another life. Well-groomed, but glaring out at the camera.

Again, the buffering completed, and no image matched.

"Shit," she said.

"AI isn't that smart I guess," Brenner said smugly, as if he'd somehow scored one for the human team.

She ignored his skepticism and initiated another search sequence. Again the search returned the same frustrating result: no hits. The man was a ghost.

"Nothing? Seriously?" Ella stepped away from the counter, crossed her arms and frowned, willing the screen to yield something, anything.

She considered the databases she had already parsed through - criminal records, international travel logs, social media footprints. She did not think she had missed a relevant search. It was as though Miles Cruise had vanished into thin air.

"Impossible!" she admonished the room's bare walls. "There has to be a trail. Everyone slips up eventually." Yet, as much as she believed in that proverb, the evidence – or lack thereof – gnawed at her. What had she overlooked?

Ella leaned in once more, her eyes scanning the list of databases yet to be searched—a list that grew shorter with each passing hour. With a deep inhale, she prepared herself for another round, refusing to let the fatigue deter her.

"Alright, Miles!" she snapped, a personal challenge laid bare in the dimly lit office. “I'm coming for you.”

She initiated another query, watching as the program sifted through countless faces, searching for any semblance of the man who haunted her every waking moment. But again, the results pane remained stubbornly empty. It was as if Miles Cruise existed only in the shadows, always one step ahead and out of reach.

"Dammit!" Ella slammed her palm against the desk, the sharp sound ricocheting off the walls. For a moment, she allowed herself to feel the full weight of her exasperation.

"Is this guy made of vapor or what?" she wondered, her internal monologue a mix of sarcasm and vexation. She could almost hear Priscilla's scathing retort, mocking her inability to catch a break in this case.

Yet, as disheartened as she felt, Ella's resolve only hardened. She would not be bested by a criminal who preyed on the innocent and vulnerable. No, she would find him, bring him to justice, and make sure that the ghosts of the women who bore his mark could rest in peace.

Ella's fingers danced again across the keyboard, with a grace that belied her growing frustration. "Okay, let's try cross-referencing facial recognition with international flight manifests... Nothing? Really? Ridiculous!"

Her breaths were measured, punctuated by the rhythmic tapping of keys as she probed deeper into the abyss of data.

"Think, Ella, there's got to be something we're missing here," she coaxed herself. Her mind flitted back to the crime scenes, the lifeless forms of the women, their skin marked not just with bruises but ink—pictures etched in flesh.

"Wait a minute," she whispered. A memory flashed: the intricate tattoos on two of the victims' bodies, beautiful and haunting.

"Display images of the victims' tattoos," Ella commanded the AI, using the voice-to-text-app on her phone. The high-resolution photographs popped up. She examined the tattoos meticulously, memorizing the pattern.

"Run a search for similar tattoos in criminal databases, social media, anything you can scour," she instructed the AI, her words slicing through the stillness of the room. "And hurry."

As the program whirred to life, Ella leaned back in her chair, her gaze unwavering from the screen. She could feel the tendrils of hope wrapping around her heart, lifting it with every passing second.

"Come on, come on," she urged under her breath. If her theory was correct, if those tattoos were the breadcrumbs leading to Miles Cruise, then she was on the verge of uncovering a trail that had remained cold for far too long.

The AI beeped, signaling the completion of the task. Ella scanned the results like Midas counting his coins. Every fiber of her being vibrated with the thrill of the chase.

Data cascaded down the screen, strings of text intermingling with pictures, but one word stood out among the rest: 'Budapest.'

"Gotcha," she whispered, a triumphant smile curving her lips.

Both the unknown women, it seemed, were from Budapest. Arrest records. She clicked on the files.

Susan Novak. Age 32. Brown hair, brown eyes, 65 inches tall. Human trafficking charges. Released three years ago.

Natalia Kovacs. Age 28. Blonde hair, brown eyes, 63 inches tall. Assault and battery charges. Currently on probation.

Ella felt a jolt of excitement. Budapest. Two women with tattoos matching those found on the victims, both with criminal records. The pieces were starting to come together, forming a clearer picture of Miles Cruise's activities.

Without wasting another moment, Ella zeroed in on Susan Novak's arrest record, her fingers flying across the keyboard as she delved deeper into the details. The report chronicled an extensive investigation that ultimately led to Novak's release due to lack of evidence. But something caught Ella's attention—a name mentioned in passing during the investigation: Viktor Petrov.

Intrigued, Ella began digging into Petrov's background, scouring public records, social media profiles, and any other digital breadcrumbs he had left behind. A portrait of a thug emerged—a man who operated in the shadows of Budapest's criminal underworld, connected to various illegal activities including human trafficking.

"Alright, Viktor," she murmured with a steely resolve. "Time for you to step into the light."

Her fingers flew across the keyboard once more, initiating a search on Viktor Petrov. Files opened on her screen.

"There," Brenner tapped an image. "Look."

She did. And she spotted them. Two smiling women, one blonde, one brunette, both staring out at the camera. Ella's heart wrenched to the faces that now belonged only to cold, frigid corpses.

But there they were. Both victims flanking Viktor Petrov...

"Shit," she said. "Petrov... doesn't look anything like Miles."

"Maybe... a client? They're clearly prostitutes, working for this Petrov guy," said Brenner, frowning.

She hesitated. "Just... one thought."

She pulled up images of the arrowheads now. The same ones they'd found back at the crime scene and that Brenner had marked as homemade.

She'd made assumptions, but now realized that those assumptions would cause trouble if she wasn't careful. She took the photos of the arrows and fed them through the same AI database.

"Is that going to work?" Brenner said.

She just shrugged, waiting patiently.

The program whirred to life, analyzing the arrow images pixel by pixel. Ella watched as the screen flickered, displaying a series of intricate patterns and symbols.

Minutes ticked by like hours until finally, a soft chime signaled completion. Ella leaned forward, her eyes scanning the results.

A single link.

Clicking on the link, Ella found herself immersed in a virtual storefront that showcased an array of unique arrowheads. Each one was painstaking handcrafted, reflecting both traditional Hungarian designs and contemporary artistry. The website belonged to a business named "Arcanum Arrows." It was owned by none other than Viktor Petrov.

Jubilation coursed through Ella's veins as she realized the significance of this discovery. Petrov, it seemed, had woven his criminal activities into a legitimate business venture. She began delving further into Arcanum Arrows, uncovering its origin and clientele.

The online presence of the shop was teeming with testimonials from satisfied customers around the world.

"Shit," she said.

"What?"

"The arrows are from Budapest too. Petrov makes them and owns the store."

"Who is this Petrov asshole?"

She hesitated. "A gangster, I think... But Brenner, what are the odds that two of the women he works with end up dead, shot with arrows his company made?"

"In Alaska? Not high."

"I... did you see anything in Cruise's file about Petrov?"

"No. But I can check."

"Let's do it."

Chapter 13

Ella frowned at the laptop screen open on her lowered tray table. Around her, the small aircraft thrummed as it cut through the clouds toward Juneau. The city lay like a secret whispered between towering mountains and the icy embrace of Gastineau Channel – a place where beauty and danger swirled around each other like the evening fog.

"Looks quiet," Brenner murmured beside her, his gaze scanning the landscape below.

"Quiet like a bear lying in wait," Ella replied, her voice low. She did not want to disturb the concentrated silence among the rest of the team behind her. Four other marshals accompanied them, all briefed on their target, each now bringing themselves up to speed.

Brenner squinted at her computer. "The intel is reliable?"

"Very," she insisted. "Petrov is in Juneau for an expo."

"For his arrows?"

"Some sort of hunting business expo." She showed him the webpage, and the airline tickets in Petrov's name she'd found.

The FBI database had flagged Petrov's name the moment she'd input it. And now, while Kogan and his fellow hunter suspects convened with legal counsel, the team of five marshals and one FBI agent descended on Juneau in search of the man who connected two of their victims and the arrows used to slay them.

The cabin pressure shifted, a perceptible sigh as the aircraft began its gradual descent into Juneau. Ella stared out the window, where the landscape below coalesced into a patchwork of greens and grays, stitched together by veins of silver rivers and the glint of a distant ocean.

"Looks like a postcard," Brenner mused beside her. He adjusted the cuff of his sleeves and ran his fingers through his dark hair, these gestures the only hints of his inward tension before a mission.

Ella flexed her fingers, feeling the familiar weight of her service weapon at her hip beneath the unassuming cut of her blue second-hand blazer. Her heartbeat throbbed with the little plane's engines.

Behind them, the four deputy marshals conferred softly, pointing out key details in the files. They were all about Ella and Brennan's age, fit and clean-cut, with ruddy complexions from the Alaskan climate. They also knew they were chess pieces poised for a gambit, as they sifted information and scenarios behind stoic exteriors.

"Arrow expo, huh?" Deputy Marshal Larkin scoffed, addressing the whole of the rumbling cabin. He had sandy hair and an open face. His tone showed he thought the whole idea was absurd, a facade for criminality.

"Every collector and enthusiast in the area will be there," Ella replied without looking away from her own window. "Petrov must be using it as a cover. He won't expect us to make a move in such a public venue."

Below, the wispy fog swayed like a curtain in a sea breeze, revealing first one portion of the city, then another. Ella knew the streets were a patchwork of history and modern struggle. Old clapboard storefronts with their colorful facades huddled together, defiant against the encroachment of newer buildings of glass and steel that grabbed for the sky.

"Which is exactly why we strike there," Brenner added. "We've got one shot at this. Once Petrov gets wind of us, he'll vanish. We can't let that happen."

"Then we won't," she said, her voice a steel edge.

"Approach is good," the pilot's voice crackled over the intercom. "Prepare for landing."

Ella fastened her seatbelt, the click a sharp punctuation in the quiet cabin. She pressed the button then put her seat fully upright. She looked up at Brenner, blue eyes into blue.

"We're bringing him down," she said, her words a vow.

The plane's wheels touched down. Ella remained relaxed as the plane bumped and juddered on the runway, swaying easily with its motion. When the plane began to coast along the runway, she shook out her hands, flinging away any last doubt. She would do this and do it well.

As they taxied to the modest airport terminal, Ella allowed herself one final moment to take in the sight of Juneau, this island town cradled by nature. The sea bordered one side, mountains the other. The only way in or out of the city was by plane or ferry.

Alaska was famously snake-less, but a viper had come to Juneau, and Ella and her team were going to snare it.

Ella stood, slung her bag over her shoulder and headed for the exit. As she deplaned to the portable stairway, a glint of sun showed through the clouds to gleam on her blonde ponytail. Brenner, towering behind her, smiled at the sight. The air smelled of salt and pine, a crispness that calmed some of her heated anticipation.

“All right, men,” she called over her shoulder to the team, “Let’s go trap that snake.” She ran down the stairs lithe as a ballerina, her eyes those of a hunter.

Ella's phone buzzed as they navigated the rental van through Juneau's streets, still slick from the recent rain. It was a text from the local PD liaison: "Petrov arrived 20 mins ago with four. Armed? Unknown. Caution advised."

"Four additional heartbeats," she murmured, her thumb hovering over the screen before locking the device and glancing at Brenner. His jaw clenched slightly.

"So, more shadows to chase, team," he announced to the men behind them, not taking his eyes off the road. As he downshifted for a traffic light, Ella could see that his leg was bothering him, that he was compensating for the stiffness with will and expert steering.

Brenner took a sharp left. The move took them to the harbor. Soon she could see the water-side hotel. Unlike similar hotels on vacation islands, this one stood like a steel fortress against the relentless waves. Ella's gaze lifted to the building. Above the ground floor, every room had its own balcony, backed by tinted plate glass windows that reflected both another hotel across the street and higher up, the gray clouds interspersed by patches of blue sky.

The hotel parking lot was off to the side. As Brenner drove slowly past, they took stock. A boardwalk ran along the marina, its slips empty this time of year. A walkway led around the side of the hotel to where the boardwalk ended in mooring spots directly abutting the back of the hotel. During the warm season, tour boats, deliveries, maybe even yachts could float right up to the hotel to disembark. Now a little ice rimmed the edge of the mooring area, and there were no boats on the open water.

"Back there's our entry point," Brenner further decelerated, and now gestured to the right where the boardwalk ended.

"Remember, Petrov is slippery. We need him breathing and talking," Ella reminded the team as they checked their weapons and equipment one last time. Her fingers curled around the grip of her own sidearm, a comforting weight against her palm.

"Breathing's optional, talking's not," Deputy Marshal Jensen, a stocky former hockey player quipped, but the humor didn't quite reach his eyes.

"Let's stick to the plan," Brenner interrupted. "Keep it clean, in and out. We're going through the back. According to local law enforcement Petrov has gunmen stationed in the only stairwell. We can't go through the front, it's too public, and the side fire door leads directly into the stairwell. For the element of surprise, we need to go through a rear, sea-facing window."

"A window? How the hell are we supposed to do that?" Jensen again. "Only way to the back side is in the water. Bit cold for a swim without wetsuits."

"Boat," Brenner said simply.

Jensen stared, then, slowly, a grin split his face, showing a chipped front tooth that gave him a piratical air. "Gonna be fun."

The car came to a halt two buildings down from the hotel, where a jetty jutted out from the boardwalk into the choppy water. At the end of the jetty, a man in a large, green puffy coat stood waiting, behind him a white, low-slung speedboat that rocked in the choppy waves. The six law enforcement officers spilled out of their vehicle, and moved as one, the four marshals following Ella and Brenner across the wet wooden decking toward the man with the keys.

Brenner took the lead. "Any more info on Petrov's team?"

"No, sir," said the cop in plainclothes. "Two gunmen on the stairs. Three men in the room, all ugly thugs. Nothing else."

Brenner nodded. He and the cop exchanged keys, and the latter trotted off to park their van somewhere inconspicuous.

"Ready?" Brenner's night-blue gaze swept hers. He knew she disliked boats. She had almost drowned once, a long time ago.

In answer, she stepped onto the deck and moved to the opposite edge, her steps rolling with the boat as though she were part of it.

Vibrations from the boat engine thrummed under Ella's feet as they veered out from Juneau's picturesque shoreline into open sea, Brenner at the wheel. He was taking a meandering route to the hotel's less conspicuous rear entrance. Sea spray misted her face, cooling the anxious heat that flushed her cheeks.

"With Petrov's men on high alert, we need the element of surprise," Brenner explained over the roar of the boat's motor. His eyes scanned the darkening horizon. Evening came early and fast at this latitude, though not as fast as in Nome. He turned the boat in a wide semi-circle back towards the city. "We slip in from the back, we control the play."

"Agreed." Ella trusted Brenner's tactical mind as much as her own instincts, which were currently screaming that this was their best shot. "We need every advantage we can get." She clutched the rail and steadied her breathing.

"Jensen, Michaels," Brenner called to the two deputy marshals positioned at the bow, their profiles etched against the fading light. "You're on exit duty. Nobody leaves that building without going through you first."

"Got it, Gunn," Jensen nodded, his hand resting on the holstered weapon at his side. He shared a look with Michaels, a pact to stand as an unyielding barrier between Petrov and any hope of escape.

As the boat neared its destination, Ella leaned forward, her eyes reflecting the steely waters below.

"Remember, no heroics," Brenner continued, voice carrying above the wind. "This is about precision, not brute force."

"Understood," Michaels, lanky and with a parrot's schnozz, adjusted his Kevlar vest snugly around his torso. He scanned the hotel, a soldier surveying battlefield terrain before a charge. Its windows picked up reflections from the sunset, flashing orange and peach and pink.

"Keep comms open and clear," Ella reminded them.

"Copy that," Larkin said, touching his earpiece in confirmation.

The boat's engine softened to a purr as they approached the shadowed dock behind the hotel. Streetlamps at either end of the hotel came on as the boat drifted in, the light reflecting off the water. The team kept silent as they prepared to disembark. Sound amplified on the water. Ella took a deep breath, steadying herself for the task ahead.

"Let's bring this bastard in," she whispered more to herself than anyone else, feeling Brenner's presence beside her. They would do this together, and they would do it right. Ella's resolve solidified with the thought; there was no room for doubt now, only action.

The Alaskan moonlight cast long, eerie shadows across the water as Ella studied the hotel's sea-facing side. The structure loomed like a monolith against the dimming sky—a stronghold guarding secrets.

She jumped on cat feet from the boat to the hotel loading dock, mooring rope in hands. Soundlessly, except for her breath, she bent and wrapped the rope around the cleat for the purpose. As she straightened, the others followed her. She moved off, still scrutinizing the hotel wall. At the end of the dock was the steel loading door which penetrated to the staircase manned by Petrov's bodyguards. Above, lights glowed in various windows.

But not in all. The local plainclothesman had already seen to that. To the left, a steel trellis climbed the wall between the first couple of balconies. The trellis was bare, waiting for spring and new vines. She tested the structure: sturdy and well-footed. She turned and gave a thumbs-up to the men behind her.

Now she began to climb, moving swiftly, pulling her petite frame up the cross-bars of the trellis.

Reaching the balconies, Ella swung herself to the left one, up and over the railing. She glided across the balcony's cement floor, to the sliding window. Ella pushed. The latch unclicked and the door slithered open along its track. She slipped inside. Soon the rest of the team joined her, ghost-like in their silence as they hovered in the narrow lanes between oversized furniture. The wind from outside chilled the room but also swept away its mustiness. Brenner brought up the rear, sliding the door closed behind him, cutting off the stinging ocean wind. They hadn't turned on a lamp, but their eyes were fully adjusted to the dim surroundings.

Padding across the carpet, Ella opened the door to the corridor and looked both ways. Not a soul.

"Clear," she whispered, and eased into the hall. The rest of the team followed, single file, not one jostling another, pros at work.

"Positions," Brenner hissed. The team dispersed. Jensen and Michaels, a tall and short odd couple, headed right, to the stairwell that led up, to Petrov's guards, and down, to the back hotel exit. Sandy-haired Larkin and his partner – Ella could not remember his name, but he had dark floppy hair, like a St. Bernard - shadowed Brenner and Ella. The plush hotel carpet muffled their footfalls.

Ella felt the weight of her pistol against her hip, a reminder of what was at stake. Petrov was here, in this hotel, and they were the hunters closing in. Her thoughts filtered a swirling mix of anticipation and the drilled-in procedures of protocol.

She led the other marshals forward, Brenner flanking her as they moved down the cramped hallway.

Notwithstanding the deep carpet, the hotel was a somewhat shabby affair, with few pictures on the wall, most of them cheaply framed prints of Alaskan mountains. The wallpaper, sage green shadows of Alaskan spruce, had begun to peel in corners. A draft indicated the need for better insulation, as did the distant sound of crashing waves. Closer at hand, Ella could hear the murmurs of guests behind some of the closed doors.

Three quarters of the way down the hall, an alcove led to an elevator. Brenner and Ella took the first lift, walking in to stand by an elderly Japanese couple who had hit the light for the seventh floor. Ella smiled as she went inside. Brenner tapped the button for three, and settled beside her, facing forward according to good elevator etiquette. Casually, he took her hand as if they too were a couple and not cops on a raid. When they exited the elevator, Ella saw the older couple exchange a knowing smile. A little regretfully, she released Brenner's hand. She thought she heard him give a quick sigh, but when she glanced over his profile was stern as ever.

316, 312, 308. Ella counted down the numbers. She heard the elevator open again and heard a brief soft rumble of male voices. Larkin and his hairy partner, their backup.

Petrov was in 304, almost in the back corner, several rooms down from the stairwell doors. When they reached 304, Brenner flattened himself at one side of the door while Ella took up her position on the other. They exchanged a brief nod, their unspoken communication affirming readiness.

They shot a glance towards the end of the hall, the top of the stairwell. Somewhere on the lower landing, two of Petrov's men were keeping an eye on things. Hopefully, the Marshal team's stealth would avoid a shootout with the goons.

And then the stairwell door clanged open.

Ella turned sharply.

A man was coming through the door, a broad man with flat features and short dirty blonde hair. He wore jeans, a black leather jacket and a golden hoop earring through his left ear. He carried a plastic tray laden with sandwiches and vending machine snacks, whistling as he strolled down the hall towards them.

Towards Petrov's door.

She didn't recognize the man, but he had the look of an Eastern European. She tensed. Brenner also froze at her side.

They'd spotted him, and it was only a matter of time before he looked up and--

His eyes found theirs.

He stopped.

The two marshals behind them had guns drawn, pointed at him.

He swallowed nervously, his gaze bouncing around.

And then, he shouted. It sounded like a warning. He flung the tray and spun on his heel, sprinting back towards the stairwell. The tray hit the wall with a crash – the outer wall of Petrov's room.

Chapter 14

Ella Porter's pulse pounded in her ears, loud as the footfall's of the man tearing down the hotel hallway. He was shouting in Hungarian, with enough volume to alert not only Room 304 but also anyone in the stairway. "Állj meg!" he screamed. His eyes, as he flung himself sideways to the door, bulged with panic above his flat cheekbones.

The tray upended on the plush carpet, a casualty of his desperate flight—a still life of scattered sandwiches and shattered porcelain.

"Damn it!" Ella pushed off from the wall, her hand moved instinctively to the gun at her hip. "Brenner, we need—"

The crack of a gunshot ripped through her words. She flinched instinctively. The bullet embedded itself in the metal fire door above the thug's head. Of course, Brenner's aim was true. The warning shot thundered in the confined space, jiggling the pictures on the wall.

"On the floor!" Brenner barked, sidestepping into the hall, his gun in a double handed grip. "Now!" His order reverberated down the corridor.

The man dove to the ground as if his limbs had turned to lead, his body thudding into the carpet. The deputy marshals swept past Ella, their movements coordinated and swift. They cuffed the man, reading his rights unceremoniously, then dragged him back down the hallway towards the elevator, even as shouting erupted in room 304.

Now Petrov and his remaining goons were mobilizing. Ella and Brenner moved into position again, guns in hand. Ella sent up a prayer that Jensen and Michaels had control of the stairwell and the guards there.

A middle-aged woman guest in 313 opened her door. She had dyed black hair teased to an amazing height, wore tight leather pants, and had a cigarette in hand. "What the hell is going on out here? I'm trying to do yoga!"

"Get back!" Ella ordered. "Find safety, now!" Her eyes scanned the surroundings for potential hazards or escape routes.

The guest slammed her door, and Ella could hear not only her, but other residents scrabbling to bolt and chain their doors.

Ella now focused on Petrov's door. Behind it, ominous thumps, shouted foreign commands and the scrape of furniture gave evidence of men building a barricade.

Ella took a deep inhale. "Federal agent!" she bawled in a voice twice her size. "Open the door immediately!"

From inside 304, a guttural shout mocked her order. It was not the sound of surrender.

Ella's hand gripped her sidearm. Brenner moved shoulder to shoulder with her. They exchanged a quick glance, silent communication perfected over countless operations, then faced the door together.

"Room 304, this is your last warning!" she bellowed. Every muscle quivered, ready to breach.

A sudden burst of gunfire echoed in the stairwell at the end of the hall. Shit! Petrov's two goons kicked open the door and burst into the corridor. They were compact, pitiless-eyed, with guns high and spitting fire.

“Contact!” Brenner barked as he swung toward the new threat.

"Marshal down!" someone yelled from behind, by the elevator alcove. Ella looked back. Larkin had slumped to the carpet, a red stain spreading across on his shirt.

"Covering fire!" Brenner's command cut through the chaos, as he squeezed off two precise shots.

The gunmen buckled, guns falling from their hands, their threats extinguished by Brenner's unerring aim. Brenner jerked his head at the remaining Marshal behind him, who came round the corner. Together they loped to the thugs on the ground.

Suddenly, Brenner whirled. "Watch out!"

His shout jolted Ella as he had intended. She became aware of what his commando hearing had already discerned, a clicking noise from inside room 304. Instincts engaged, Ella lunged, tackling Brenner to the ground an instant before the door exploded in a shower of splinters and machine gun fire.

"Down!" she yelled, her command punctuated by the rat-tat-tat of bullets seeking flesh. Wood chips flew like deadly confetti, embedding themselves into walls and anything—or anyone—in their path.

"Stay down," Ella ordered through clenched teeth, pulling Brenner closer to the relative safety of the wall. The stench of gunpowder filled her nostrils, a bitter reminder of the thin line between life and death.

For a moment, nothing but the ping of bullets hitting walls and floor echoed through the hallway. Time slowed for those few fleeting seconds, all their lives hanging in balance, trapped between life and death.

Ella's tension bubbled up into a need to act. The gunmen from inside room 304 continued to spray bullets indiscriminately. It was only a matter of time before another Marshal or a guest in the hotel got hit.

As if the thought conjured reality, at that instant the stairwell door opened again, and Jensen and Michaels hurtled into the corridor. They skidded to a stop as they saw the extent of the bullet spray. Jensen dove behind a tall fake Ficus tree in an oversized pot. Michaels ducked into a niche by the elevator. A second later, a steel utility cart rolled out in the hall, a moving shield for the lanky Marshal. Ella could see his beaky nose every time he leaned to the side to train a shot at door 304.

"Cover me!" she yelled to Brenner, her voice almost drowned by the staccato symphony of bullets. The Marshals were inching closer. Jensen clutched at his arm, where a ricocheting bullet had left a gash. Larkin had pulled himself back into the elevator nook, but his fuzzy partner was on the ground, crawling forward military style to join Brenner.

"Moving!" Brenner called back, his hand signaling the scattered agents to lay down covering fire. He crossed the threshold of the door, going low against the wall.

"Going around!" she replied, her decision made. In a low crouch, she dashed toward a hotel room door—308, to be exact—further down from the chaos, her heart thudding against her ribcage.

"Damn it, Ella! Wait for—" Brenner's protest was cut short as she slammed her shoulder against the door of 308, hurtling into the room, slamming the door behind her.

Her ears rang with the sudden quiet.

She allowed herself the barest moment to catch her breath, her thoughts a whirlwind. 'Outmaneuver them,' she reminded herself.

The room was dim, curtains drawn tight, but Ella's eyes quickly adjusted. She moved like a wraith, her footsteps silent on the carpet. Every second mattered, every movement had to count.

"Be ready," she whispered into her comm, knowing Brenner would hear. She shifted her gun into her right hand as she approached the sliding door to the balcony.

A swift tug unlocked the door. She hauled it open, also jerking the curtain aside. Cold night air flooded in along with the growl of the ocean. Above, clouds hid any stars in the sky. She allowed herself an instant of satisfaction. She had circled around; now she had the advantage.

Ella peeked out over the balcony. A sheer drop fell away from the railing directly over the marina water, churning below her with the incoming tide. To her left, the neon lights of Juneau marked the boundary between sea and land. The cold wind nipped at her cheeks, but she suppressed the shiver. She had done similar maneuvers during training. Now it was time to see if they worked in practice under lethal circumstances.

"Stay sharp," she murmured into the comm, her calm voice belying the adrenaline coursing through her veins. "I'm on the move."

She slipped onto the balcony, keeping low, her movements as fluid as shadow. One hand clutched her gun, the other braced against the icy railing as she edged along. Her eyes scanned for threats, her senses heightened to catch the slightest sound—a whisper, a footstep, the softest breath.

"Room 308 balcony is clear," Ella reported, her words barely above a whisper. "Next room looks dark. Advancing to 306."

The next balcony was only a foot and half distant from where she stood. Craning over the railing, she could see that its door was ajar, curtains fluttering like ghosts in the wind. She waited, heart pounding, listening for telltale signs of movement within. Nothing. A non-eco-conscious guest had gone out to dinner, maybe, leaving the door to the elements wide open. With a practiced grace, she swung herself over the balcony of 308, stepped across to that of 306, vaulted over the railing there. As soon as she landed, she crouched behind the cover of a plastic potted plant, its leaves rustling softly against her cheek.

Still no noise from within. Good. "306 secured. Making final approach."

The gap between the next two balconies was larger than the previous one had been, at least six feet. Her stomach twisted nervously as she eyed the slippery ice along the rail.

Using the molding around the sliding doors for balance, Ella climbed up onto the railing of balcony 306. The wind had conveniently paused, for which she was grateful. But there was no time to dawdle. She holstered her weapon to give herself full mobility. Still gripping the molding, she tensed her quads, flexed her knees, and jumped.

A rush of wind whipped past her ears as she soared through the frigid air. For a moment, she seemed to hover in the void. Then she came down, her foot hit the rail, and slipped. The ice refused purchase, she cursed, and her head struck metal. It took everything to retain her grip with her right hand as she tumbled. Her arm nearly yanked from its socket as she dangled over the slick railing, feet kicking above the icy water below.

Her heart hammered as she fought to regain control. Ella summoned every ounce of strength and lifted herself up until her hips rested on the railing. The cold metal seared her fingers, but she swung her leg up. Despite the pain, she was able to get one leg over the railing, straddling it like a horse, and then the other. She sank to the balcony floor, gasping for breath, each inhalation a relief.

She took a moment to collect herself. As her breathing subsided, she heard again the echoes of gunshots, coming from the room beyond the balcony. The intensity of the situation had not lessened; she needed to continue moving. It was a miracle that the gunfire had covered the sound of her arrival.

Ella stood up, taking a deep, calming breath before launching into action. Her boot connected with the glass door of room 304, the sound exploding into the night. Glass shattered, shards glittering like ice crystals as they scattered across the floor inside.

"Federal agent!" Her Glock was in her hands, her stance solid.

A figure whirled around from where he'd been crouching by a sofa, machine gun in hand. His eyes, wide with surprise, met hers for a fleeting moment before she squeezed her trigger. But he'd reacted faster than she'd expected, suggesting Petrov hired only the best for his personal security.

He lunged towards her, even as she squeezed off the shot. He slammed into her, sending her tumbling towards the rail. Her back hit the cold metal barrier, and the man's fingers scraped for her throat.

He smelled of alcohol and cigarettes, but his muscles bunched under his many layers were like a python's coils.

Ella twisted and pulled, trying to break his hold. The icy balcony beneath her feet offered little in the way of stability. She clawed at his forearms, his hands, squirming to escape his grip. Her gloves fell off in the struggle, so she dug her nails into the skin of his wrist.

Her assailant, a scowling, bulging brute, didn't flinch. He had a nose previously broken and a scar across his black bristling eyebrows. One of his huge hands wrapped around her windpipe. With the other, he began to raise his machine gun.

She gasped and choked, bucking to try and find better footing. It wasn't working. He smiled, a grin that showed a front gold tooth. "You die," he said.

The words ignited Ella to fury. With all her strength, she shoved her hands claws first at his eyes. He howled in pain, easing his grip enough that she could spiral away. But he grabbed her again almost immediately, rage now in his eyes too. They both hung precariously against the balcony, the cold wind howling around them.

Ella knew she was outmatched in strength. But not in agility. With a swift, calculated movement, she thrust her body against the gun, pushing it downwards. His free arm grabbed her in a bear hug, pressing her sideways against the rail. She thought a rib might break. In a movement of sheer audacity, she seized her chance. She hooked her foot behind his, and as he lunged at her she used his momentum against him. He flipped over the balcony railing.

For a fleeting second, Ella thought it was over and headed for the door. But the man's hand shot out, scrabbling for the rail, his fingers clinging on for dear life. His face, twisted in rage and surprise, was a portrait of a man who knew he had underestimated his opponent.

He scrambled back, hauling himself onto the slick balcony.

Ella approached cautiously, ready to end the confrontation. But the thug lashed out. He slipped on the ice, his body flailing wildly, and in a last-ditch effort, he reached for Ella, attempting to drag her over the edge with him.

The ensuing tussle was a blur of arms and legs, a perilous ballet on the glassy surface. Ella's heart raced as she fought for control. And then, with a sudden burst of strength born of adrenaline and fear, she knocked him down, his grip loosening as he slid across the balcony, coming to a stop inches from the edge.

The man glared up at her, but just then, she heard footsteps.

Behind her.

She whirled around, but too slow.

She saw the face of Victor Petrov. He smiled at her.

Then his hands slammed into her flank, launching her.

She reached out, shouting as she fell. She snagged the jacket of the thug. The two of them toppled over the railing, plunging towards the freezing water below.

Chapter 15

She hit the water and the shock of the cold slammed into her whole body, stopping her breath, pausing her heart.

Then she was splashing towards the surface, gulping in air.

She only had two minutes. Only two minutes before hypothermia set in. She had to get out. But these thoughts jarred with her body screaming against the cold. And the thug still had hold of her.

The frigid Alaskan waters clawed at her flesh like a thousand icy needles, each wave of the sea an assault on her will to survive. Her blonde hair, usually vibrant and full of life, now lay plastered against her scalp, strands whipping around her face like seaweed.

The water infiltrated every fiber of her clothing, dragging her down. Her body was an iceberg, numb and clumsy, yet she had to fight against the ocean's freezing embrace.

Two minutes. She had to get out of the water. Only two minutes.

Despite the paralyzing cold, Ella forced herself to kick harder, driving each stroke with a ferocity born of desperation. Her eyes, wide and alert beneath wet lashes, sought the shore. It wasn't that far away, maybe 50 yards, but her arms and legs would not cooperate. With every stroke, they seemed heavier, clumsier. Instead of getting closer, the shore seemed more and more impossible to reach. Her lungs could hardly take in air, and yet they burned.

The wind howled like a pack of wolves, taunting her efforts.

A hard grip clamped on to her ankle. The bulldog face of the thug rose in the water behind her, fingers wrapped around her foot. Her heart stalled, a single beat suspended in time.

"Let go!" Ella tried to scream, but her voice barely carried over the waves.

The grip tightened, pulling her back, and she felt her progress being undone. Panic clawed at her throat as she was yanked backwards, the shore slipping away before her very eyes.

She gasped for air. The man's silence was more terrifying than any words he could have spoken. He was the embodiment of her nightmares, the menace always lingering at the edge of her mind whenever she went near the water. And now she was in the water, and the nightmare was real, not a dream.

The chill of the water threatened to lock her muscles. She could feel the man's fingers digging into the flesh of her ankle, a vice of malice. Panic fluttered in her chest like a caged bird, but she pushed it down. No! She was an FBI agent, made of sterner stuff.

Ella angled her free leg, drawing on every ounce of trembling agility she had left. Her mind flashed to countless hours spent in training, the grueling self-defense classes that had seemed excessive at the time. Now, they were her salvation.

With a sudden, explosive motion, she launched her heel upwards and felt it connect with something solid – the man's face.

His grip slackened.

Seizing the opportunity, Ella contorted her body like a dolphin. Water resistance turned into an advantage as she used it to wrench her leg free. A surge of triumph ran through her veins.

Now she kicked hard with both legs, propelling herself forward. It was enough to leave the thug behind, but now she had to get to shore.

Usually after exertion, Ella's muscles burned, her heart thumped hard enough to bang her rib cage. But this was different. Her heart was slowing, her lungs pressing in on it. For warmth? Or to hide from the chill air? Her muscles didn't hurt, her legs had become blocks of lead, her arms deadened logs. She wanted to fall asleep. Only the lights from the shore kept her going.

But she could feel Petrov's muscle-man behind her, his presence a shark fin cutting through the water, identifying her as prey. Ella could almost feel his fingers trailing in the wake of her thrashing limbs, reaching out to drag her down.

Panic lashed at her composure, weaving through her thoughts like poison ivy. She couldn't let fear paralyze her—not when she had come this far, not when she still had work to do.

Her strokes grew more frantic and less effectual. The shore was close—so close she could almost feel the gritty wooden dock beneath her fingertips. But so was the thug, his anger another force frothing the water.

She felt him snag at her again. And this time, something sharp slashed across her leg. She rolled onto her back to see him. He wielded a knife.

The idiot was going to get them both killed. The cold wasn't a respecter of persons.

He wasn't giving her a choice. He raised his knife to stab again, and she turned sharply, reaching out and catching his wrist with fingers that felt like the hands of a rag doll. But they were strong enough, apparently. She twisted, disarming him and snagging the knife.

The man blinked in surprise, but she shoved off him again, this time by burying the knife into his arm.

He bellowed in pain as she kicked off him. The incoming tide pushed her the last few yards to the dock. Her trembling fingers found purchase in the wood. Shivering violently, she pulled herself from the water and collapsed onto the damp planks. She felt her heart pick up its pace again. Her lungs unclenched, demanding air. She gulped it in, her skin and muscles screaming in protest as numbed nerves reawakened.

She couldn't stay long in this state. Her clothes would freeze to her skin. With sheer force of will, she pushed herself up. She had to grit her teeth against the pain and the convulsive shivering. Her legs shaking, she stumbled forward.

She glanced behind her, seeing the man thrashing in the water, already too far to reach. He had been stopped by the cold, but she knew he was not dead. His death would not be her responsibility. He was drifting out to sea, and his head disappeared under the waves.

Then he was gone.

Ella stumbled away from the hotel across the parking lots. She was looking for their SUV and she could not see it.

She took a moment to catch her breath, trying to calm her spinning thoughts even while her body continued its convulsive trembling. She couldn't afford to let panic rule her. She couldn't afford to let fear control her actions.

She needed to get warm. Now.

Her earpiece was soaked. No communication was possible. The car they'd come in had emergency packs in the back. Clothes. Blankets. Warming packs. She lurched along the boardwalk, teeth chattering horribly.

She saw the car in the second lot beyond the jetty, in a near corner. Thanking God, she shuffled toward it, fumbling in her pocket for the spare key.

She felt she was losing sensation in her fingers and toes, as if they were turning into ice, but she knew she couldn't afford to dwell on that. Her mission was do or die, and she had no intention of dying.

She clicked the locks and opened the hatch. She rummaged through the supplies, finding dry clothing and a blanket. She grabbed them and crawled into the driver seat. The remote signal from the key allowed her to start the engine. Once it was going, she put the car into neutral, engaged the parking brake, and turned on the heater. Then, uncaring of modesty, she peeled off her saturated clothing with shaking fingers and replaced them with warm layers. Wrapping the blanket tightly around her body, she huddled against the cold, waiting for the heat to blast and warm up her body.

The adrenaline that fueled her escape had drained from her system, leaving her exhausted and shaken. She closed her eyes, trying to block out the world and focus on her breathing. It was the only thing keeping her grounded in that moment. That, and the heat now blowing out of the vents onto her face.

As warmth started to seep back into her, Ella heard the faint sound of radio static.

"Ella. Ella, we have Petrov. Where are you?"

She felt a flicker of relief, staring towards the radio on the dash.

They had him. They had their suspect... now, they needed to find out if he was the one behind the murders.

Chapter 16

The chill of the Alaskan sea clung to Ella Porter like a second skin, leaving her shivering even in the warmth of the Juneau interrogation room. It was a stark place, all harsh fluorescent lighting and walls devoid of comfort or color. A single table sat anchored in the center, as unyielding as the handcuffs resting upon them.

"Mr. Petrov," she began, a little irritated that she had to control the tremble in her voice—not from fear, but from cold. "You know why you're here."

Petrov—a bear of a man with steel in his gaze—merely shrugged.

"Come on, Petrov," Ella pressed, rubbing her arms for warmth, her eyes fixed intently on him. "This charade isn't necessary."

He mumbled, the Russian rolling off his tongue. But he wasn't a great actor, his eyes when she spoke flickered with understanding. He knew English, the liar.

Ella leaned forward, her hair falling over her shoulders in a cascade of gold. Her feet still felt numb, and she could feel Brenner's eyes on her.

He'd wanted to go solo on this, let her rest. But she'd lied to him. She'd told him she'd accidentally gotten a bit wet. She hadn't mentioned the battle in the frigid sea.

Now, though, he watched her intently from his vantage point against the side wall and she tried not to glance in his direction.

"I've seen your file. Budapest, Moscow, Prague... You're a long way from home, Petrov."

His stoic facade wavered for a moment, then set again. The temperature in the room seemed to drop further, tension settling like a cold front. Ella's teeth chattered slightly, but she held his gaze, refusing to look away or show any other signs of weakness.

"Fine," she conceded. "Don't talk now. But we both know you'll have to speak eventually. And I can wait." She leaned back, proving her point.

She was surprised when Brenner used the pause to exit the room but didn't let it show. She simply sat, staring at Petrov. He was a bulky man, with coarse brown hair, deep-set black eyes, and no neck on those thick shoulders. He'd been wearing a rust cashmere crew-neck sweater when they brought him in, but now he sat in dingy jailhouse grays. It's what happened when you were accused of attempted murder.

He looked away first. She just kept staring, biding her time.

When the door opened again, she wasn't surprised to see Brenner come back in. She was surprised that he had a steaming mug of tea in hand, US Marshal printed on its white surface. He brought it over to the table and set it by her hand, then resumed his lounging against the wall.

Ella pulled the mug closer, wrapping her fingers around its warmth. A sudden memory surfaced, Kerry Lonegan in the Nome Marshal's office, wrapped in a blanket, nursing a hot cup of cocoa. The difference was, Kerry had been abducted. Ella had helped take down this criminal.

She took a sip of the tea – orange spice, with a little honey. It warmed her throat and gullet, and she could feel the shivering subside as the liquid went down. She put down the mug and scraped her chair forward.

"Let's try something different." She opened the file in front of her and reached for the stack of photographs. The glossy pictures of the winter scene where they'd found the bodies had only one pop of color – the crimson blood on the snow and on the women's faces.

Brenner's hand twitched against the chair rail as he watched Petrov. His former Navy Seal training kept him alert for the slightest hint of violence.

"Look at these," Ella commanded, pushing the photographs across the table towards Petrov. Each image captured a life stolen. There were three, first the redhead, Emma. Then the blonde, Susan. Then the brunette, Natalia.

Petrov glanced over Emma's photograph without emotion. But when he saw those of Natalia and Susan, his reaction was not one Ella anticipated. It was not guilt that flashed across his rugged features, but an unmistakable flare of outrage.

"See something you recognize?" Ella probed. She could feel her pulse rate increase. They were onto something.

Brenner leaned forward from the wall slightly. He studied Petrov's face with the precision of a marksman sighting his target, searching for the involuntary twitches that would betray the inner workings of the man's mind.

Petrov's jaw tensed, his hands clenching into fists before he forced them to relax onto the table and donned his granite look again. It was too late, though. Ella and Brenner had glimpsed a crack in his armor, a crack that they could now wedge open.

"Outrage, Mr. Petrov? Not remorse?" Ella pressed, locking eyes with him. "Were they more than just faces to you?"

Ella eyed the pictures fanned across the industrial table like a hand of playing cards dealt from death's own deck. In her mind, she pictured the three bodies under the blue tarp. She pictured the tracking devices attached to the women's ankles.

"Mine," Petrov growled suddenly, his accent thick and rough as he jabbed a finger at the glossy images. "They work for me! They *my* girls."

His outburst sliced through the sterile quiet of the interrogation room. Ella and Brener studied him, noting that he vibrated with emotion.

"Worked for you?" Brenner's voice provided a calm counterpoint to Petrov's volatility.

"Da, mine!" Petrov spat again, his eyes flashing with something Ella couldn't quite decipher—a cocktail of possession, fury, and perhaps fear?

"Care to elaborate on that, Mr. Petrov?" Ella asked, craning forward slightly. Her fingers rested against the cold steel of the table.

Petrov clenched his jaw, his eyes flicking up and down, between the pictures on the table and the two agents before him. He leaned back in his chair as if distancing himself from the question, and by extension, the truth.

"Girls have many works," he muttered evasively, his gaze settling somewhere over Ella's shoulder, avoiding her scrutiny.

"Many works," Ella echoed, mostly to herself. The vague answer bedeviled her, the ambiguity a dark cloud of possibilities. Trafficking? Espionage?

Brenner sauntered to the table, hanging over Petrov. "Did they disappoint you? Is that why we found them this way?" Brenner prodded, using the closed tip of his pen to push the photo of Natalia closer to Petrov.

"No!" The words burst from Petrov. His deep-set eyes looked honestly shocked. "Not my doing."

"Then help us understand," Ella urged, folding her hands in front of her, making a show of calm. "What exactly did they do for you?"

Petrov's gaze darted to the door, a silent calculation playing out behind his guarded facade. He swallowed hard, a muscle flickering in his cheek.

"Mr. Petrov," Ella pressed, "the more we know, the better we can—"

"Business," he snapped, cutting her off. "Private business."

"Which is now our business," Brenner retorted, equally firm, "because you shot up a hotel and wounded two agents."

Petrov looked indifferent to the charges. "Private," he repeated, his lips curling around the word as though it were a shield.

Ella exchanged a glance with Brenner, thoughts stirring. Whatever these girls were involved in, whatever Petrov had them doing—it was clear he wasn't going to tell them without a fight. She noted the way he avoided specifics, how his body language screamed defensiveness. Ella leaned forward, studying every nuance of his position, every pore and broken vein on his skin, sifting through the layers of his deceit.

"Let's cut to the chase, Mr. Petrov," Ella said briskly. "Why come all the way to Juneau? What's at the bowhunter expo?"

Petrov's eyes flickered. He turned slightly in his chair, facing Ella again.

"Is not just show for hunting," he grunted, his accent heavy. "Is personal."

"Personal?" Brenner echoed, limping slightly as he moved around the table to stand beside Ella, a united front. The scar at his jawline twitched.

"Da," Petrov confirmed, the word sharp like the crack of a rifle in the silence. "He take my girls—two of my girls—and I track him here, to Alaska."

"Your girls?" Ella pressed, not missing the proprietary claim in his tone. "What did he do with them?"

"Stole them!" Petrov slammed a hand down on the steel surface, making both agents flinch. "I find him. I get them back."

"Stole them how?" Brenner asked.

"Is not simple," Petrov spat, his eyes blazing now. "He lure them away. Promise better life, then poof," he gestured with a flap of his hand, "gone!"

"And who lured them away?" Ella pushed. "What was his name?"

He glared at her. "Miles Cruise."

There it was again. The name of the poacher. Someone the FBI and the Marshals wanted. And no wonder... with ties to organized crime? Three murders to his name... at least.

"Is Cruise at the expo now?" Ella's pulse thrummed in her veins, each beat emphasizing the importance of her question.

"Da, he will be there." Petrov leaned forward, making sure his interlocutors understood him "And I want be waiting for him. He regret crossing me."

Ella didn't need to glance at Brenner to translate Petrov's meaning. They'd seen men like Petrov before, driven by vendettas and violence. But they also knew the danger that men like Miles Cruise presented—not just to the victims but to anyone who got in their way.

"Let's see if your story checks out, Petrov," she said finally. "But remember, you're in our territory now. And we don't play by your rules."

Petrov smirked, a glint of something dark and unrepentant in his eyes.

"Rules," he muttered, almost to himself. "Always changeable when hunting big game."

Ella's spine stiffened; she recognized the challenge.

"What do you know about Miles Cruise?" she insisted.

He shrugged.

"You want him to pay, right? Well... here's your chance. Your men are dead or in the hospital, and you're not going anywhere anytime soon. The best bet you have is for us to arrest him."

He sneered, clearly not impressed by this offer, and began to pick at his thumbnail.

"The best bet?" Petrov scoffed. "Arrest him? And let him rot in cell while my girls suffered?" He scoffed again. "He take what mine." His accent seemed to be getting heavier the angrier he grew. "I let him? No. NO!"

Ella studied the fury burning in Petrov's eyes. The man was a ticking time bomb. Defusing him wouldn't be easy. She exchanged another glance with Brenner, one that urged him to keep his own composure.

"Mr. Petrov," Ella said calmly. "We want justice just as much as you do. But taking matters into your own hands will only escalate the situation further."

Petrov leaned back in his chair and crossed his arms, a bitter smile playing at the corner of his lips. "Justice? You think him behind bars is enough for his crimes?"

Ella sighed, the weight of the situation pressing against her chest. "I understand you're angry, Mr. Petrov. And I understand why you would want to take matters into your own hands. But there are ways to ensure that he pays."

Petrov's eyes narrowed, his expression a mix of defiance and despair. It was clear that reason alone wouldn't sway him.

"You no understand," he growled. "This man... he's... bastard. Evil!"

"Tell us everything you know about Cruise," Brenner interjected, guiding Petrov. "How did he first approach you?"

"The Wolf," Petrov said simply.

"Excuse me?"

"Cruise... his bodyguard. The Wolf. His name. They say, da?"

"I'm confused. The Wolf? This is a known associate of his?" Ella asked.

Brenner was already on his phone, searching Miles Cruise's known contacts.

She waited a second, glanced over, but Brenner just shook his head.

"This... Wolf," Ella said. "Describe him."

"Big. Wear fur." Petrov frowned now, his voice shaking with something... close to fear.

"Big and wearing fur?" Ella repeated, struggling to connect the dots. "Is he some kind of bodyguard?"

Petrov hesitated before he spoke. "Is... more than guard. The Wolf, he is... how you say... enforcer. He protect Cruise, yes, but he also... ensure loyalty. Punish people who cross Cruise. Men too, but especially girls. The Wolf, he like killing. Does not care who. He just like killing."

Ella's heart sank at Petrov's revelation.

"Did your girls ever mention anything about the Wolf?" Ella could see her own horror in the way Brenner's scar pulsed.

Petrov shook his head. His wide mouth curled down, a rictus of emotional pain. "No... They were too afraid... Stayed away. Before he took them."

"Also, he... sniper," added Petrov, his voice flat.

"Excuse me?" Ella said, surprised.

"He sniper," Petrov insisted more firmly.

"This Wolf?"

"Da."

"What sort of sniper?" Brenner asked, leaning in.

"Brilliant sniper. He... he hit a target from mile away," Petrov responded, his voice barely above a whisper. "I see. I see him do."

Ella felt a shiver crawl down her spine. More pieces fell into place, forming a picture of the man they were up against. Miles Cruise, a vicious criminal with ties to organized crime, and his enforcer, a serial murderer, known as the Wolf.

"Does this Wolf only use a rifle?" asked Ella. It nagged at her, that the women had all been killed with arrows. Was Petrov trying to deflect suspicion from himself, the real artist of fletching?

"Cruise like arrows. That how we meet," said Petrov. "He teach Wolf. Now Wolf better than Cruise. He kill deer with arrow. He kill bear with arrow." He tapped the pictures of Natalia and Susan. "Now my women die, killed with arrow that I make." He bowed his head. His shoulders trembled, and Ella realized he was grieving.

She turned to Brenner. "We need to find out more about this Wolf," Ella decided. "If he truly is Cruise's enforcer, then he must have some connection to these murders."

Brenner tilted his head to the side so that his dark hair flopped on his forehead, nodding in agreement. "We'll dig deeper into Cruise's associates and known contacts, see if we can find any leads on this Wolf." He shifted to face the crime boss across the table. "But right now, Petrov, we need you to cooperate fully with us."

Petrov's eyes flickered with a mixture of apprehension. "I no kill my women." He pointed at the stack of pictures.

"Well, you're not going anywhere for a while," Brenner said. "Believe it or not, you're not allowed to post armed guards on stairwells, or shoot at federal officers."

Or push an FBI agent off a balcony, Ella added silently.

Brenner and Ella pushed to their feet.

"Where is this expo taking place?" Ella asked.

Petrov huffed, but then shrugged. "I show." He clicked his fingers for where his phone sat in a plastic Tupperware bowl behind them, one of the old green lettuce containers from the 1980s. Clearly, this Marshal's officer needed to update its supply cabinet.

Ella got up to retrieve the device. She motioned to the mirror on the wall, and a few seconds later a uniformed officer entered the interrogation room. She handed the phone to the newcomer. "Hold this for Mr. Petrov."

The officer did so, and Petrov unlocked the device with his thumb.

Petrov scrolled through his phone, searching for the information they needed. Ella couldn't help but notice the scars that lined his hands, remnants of a violent past. It was a reminder of the darkness they were delving into.

Finally, Petrov found what he was looking for and paused the screen on an image. He motioned to the officer to give the phone back to Ella. "Expo is in warehouse area," he said, his voice tinged with bitterness. "It's where Cruise likes to make deals. He thinks he safe."

Ella studied the address on the screen and quickly jotted it down in her notepad. "Thank you, Mr. Petrov," she said sincerely. "We'll do everything we can to bring justice for Natalia and Susan."

He just snorted, crossed his arms and watched sullenly as Ella and Brenner hastened out of the interrogation room. But when Ella passed by the viewing window, she saw him brush his meaty fingers over his wet eyes.

Chapter 17

The afternoon sun slanted across the warehouse district of Juneau, casting elongated shadows across the rough asphalt. Here the snow was pushed back from the lots, lanes and walkways into big lumpy drifts, gray with dirt except where the sunlight flashed off a broken dagger of ice. Ella Porter squinted against the glare, her blue eyes reflecting a sky so clear it felt like a taunt, considering the murkiness of the task at hand. As she walked she scanned the area, noting entries and exits for vehicles and people, doors that were boarded and ones standing wide open, loading docks and office fronts.

"Quite the busy beehive," she thought. The sunshine glinted off the myriad trucks that were as much a staple here as the warehouses themselves. Four-wheel drives with mud-streaked sides, pickups with beds full of gear, and several larger rigs bearing logos of outdoor brands formed an irregular metal forest. Each one seemed to wear its dents and scrapes like badges of honor, proof of thriving in the embrace of Alaska's untamed wilderness.

Colorful trailers ringed the central parking lot, a winter wagon train marked with logos and awnings advertising custom goods, T-shirts, and hunting hats. Wooden easel signs beckoned pedestrians into various warehouses for weapons shows, the latest in hunting fashion, and ammo. Trappers haggled over prices for pelts that would later adorn the homes of those who understood little of the wilderness that provided them.

Ella paused to watch a group of hunters, their camouflage gear muddy at the hems, as they loaded up their trucks with equipment that gleamed with lethal promise. Fishermen, faces weather-beaten and hands calloused, weaved through the crowd. Occasionally their raucous laughter sliced through the air, sharp as the knives they carried.

"Looks like everyone and their dog decided to show up," Ella muttered to Brenner, as she navigated their unmarked SUV through the warehouse lots. It was as though the trucks themselves were gathered for some grand convention, whispering tales of adventure and survival amongst themselves.

"Or just anyone with a bow and something to prove," Brenner drawled, a little bored. His focus was on the mission, not the expo itself.

Ella brought the SUV to a stop behind a large, gray warehouse. They were on a side street, away from the main thoroughfare where families and enthusiasts clogged the road, streaming towards the bowhunting expo. Backup would join them shortly.

Ella killed the engine and considered Brenner, observing the way a shaft of sunshine caught the edges of his jaw, throwing the scar that traced his cheek into relief. "Alright, we're here. Remember, eyes open, no heroics."

"Wouldn't dream of it," he replied dryly, "although considering your antics at the hotel, you seem to be the one who needs that advice, not me." His faint smile took the sting from his words, but the tightness around his eyes showed he wasn't just joking. He reached for his door and eased out, the movement constrained by the old injury that never healed quite right. Standing on the sidewalk, he massaged his thigh. "We blend in, gather intel. We find Cruise and The Wolf before they realize the Marshals are onto them."

"Right." Ella's hand went to the door handle, closing around the cool metal. Her mind was already jumping ahead through the afternoon, playing out scenarios, mapping escape routes, identifying potential threats. She felt the familiar adrenaline surge, the clarity that came with it.

"Stay close," Brenner said softly as they walked away from the SUV.

Ella nodded. She wore a borrowed black jacket a little too large for her – her own was still wet from her ocean swim. Even the smallest of the Juneau Marshals was six inches taller and a few dozen pounds heavier than she, so she rather felt like a child trying on one of her father's big sweaters for dress-up.

Grief pierced her as she realized it had been nearly a day since she had thought of him, so consumed had she become by the case. Then it occurred to her that he, with his own obsession for his company and position, would have understood. She wasn't sure what to make of that thought.

Mentally she shook herself and returned to the task at hand. Under her jacket, she felt the weight of her concealed weapon against her hip. She pulled gloves from her pocket and put them on, all the while scanning her surroundings. Steel storage sheds hulked on either side of the street, doors shut and padlocked. So far, no people wandered about in this area.

A pair of nondescript sedans slid into the empty space behind Ella and Brenner's SUV. With synchronized precision, doors opened, and six local cops spilled out onto the concrete. Clad in body armor, they looked like warriors spilling out from the Trojan horse.

"Alright, listen up," Brenner raised his voice a little so they could all hear. He stood before the crew, his stance firm.

"Inside these walls," Brenner continued, gesturing towards the warehouse with a scarred hand, "is a viper's nest. Miles Cruise and his heavy, known as The Wolf, are no strangers to violence." His gaze locked onto each person in turn. "These men are cornered animals, and they will lash out if given a chance."

Ella watched the officers nod, faces set. Memories of past briefings flickered behind her eyes—times when the danger had been just as palpable, the stakes just as high.

"Keep your heads on a swivel," Brenner continued. "Cruise is cunning, resourceful. And The Wolf... he's earned his moniker. He likes to kill. Don't underestimate him."

"Understood," came the collective murmur from the team. Ella felt the familiar itch, the readiness that sang in her veins. It was more than training; it was instinct honed over countless missions, a symphony of muscle memory and mental preparation.

"All right." Brenner, too, was tapping his holster. "Move out!"

The Wolf was a sniper... A long-distance marksman. Brenner had spent multiple tours as a sniper himself. His moniker: the Guardian Angel, a sniper so deadly, he still didn't talk with her about his past.

Somehow, knowing this enforcer of Cruise's was also a shooter discomfited Ella, as if they'd sacrificed one advantage of their own.

She shivered, hands tense on her weapon as the group of eight moved from behind the gray warehouse. They split off, two at a time.

"Don't engage," Brenner warned into the comms. "Not until we've identified. Then call backup. Clear?"

Heads nodded. Cops fanned out.

Ella and Brenner emerged last, heading into the main area of the expo, which stretched between the old, worn buildings now bedecked in advertisements and temporary signs. The air buzzed with the energy of the crowd, a mix of eager enthusiasts and curious onlookers.

Ella and Brenner melted into the sea of parkas, many of them camouflage, blending seamlessly among the archers, hunters, and outdoor enthusiasts flowing into the maze of stalls and booths. Camouflage patterns adorned every corner, blending with the earthy tones of the surroundings. Ella couldn't help but admire the craftsmanship of some of the bows displayed, their sleek designs seemingly begging to be wielded by skilled hands. Meanwhile, she scanned constantly for any sign of Cruise and his Wolf.

As they wove through the crowd, a gathering grabbed her attention. She tapped Brenner on the arm and tilted her head to the left. He paused to look, too.

A group of hunters huddled around a makeshift shooting range, their expressions a mixture of awe and camaraderie. Ella and Brenner left the crowd to head towards the assembly.

The range consisted of various targets set at different distances, challenging participants to display their skill. The crowd watched without speaking. When Ella joined the audience, she could hear the thunk of arrows hitting sandbag targets.

A new archer stepped forward, his tall stature and bright red hair commanding attention. He wore a green camo shirt and jeans over work boots, his bow slung over his shoulder. Once in place, he drew his bow with practiced ease, his muscles rippling the material of his shirt. With unwavering focus, he released the arrow, and it soared through the air before striking dead center in the bullseye.

The crowd erupted into applause and cheers. Ella clapped too, admiring his proficiency.

The man turned around, holding the bow up. "See, what separates this beauty from the competition," he began, "is the use of the latest engineering marvels, forged by skilled craftsmen dedicated to perfecting the art of archery. The balance, the weight, and the responsiveness all give it unparalleled accuracy and precision. If there's one thing I know, it's archery, and trust me when I say you won't find a better bow on the market."

Just as he was about to continue his pitch, a sudden commotion interrupted. The noise came from back toward the main thoroughfare, people shouting, not in cheers or applause.

Ella stepped away from the archery audience, Brenner at her side "That doesn't sound good," she said, her tone low.

Brenner nodded. His eyes scanned above the sea of heads.

"See anything?"

He shook his head. "Not from here." They began to jog in the direction of the noise.

As they listened, the tumult grew louder. More shouts, a cry of fear, "A bear! He's going to kill him!"

Two other officers had noticed the commotion and were moving out of the open lot parallel to Brenner and Ella, in the direction of the sounds. They converged with Ella and Brenner on the street, where the crowd of expo-goers had stopped.

All faced a warehouse across the street, gray like all the rest, but with windows on its upper levels and scarlet streaks of graffiti adorning its walls. In one of the second floor windows, Ella could see two figures. One was definitely a man, of middle height and compact, with the stance of a former soldier. The other loomed like a bear. A large gray bear. But what was a glacier bear doing unconstrained in a warehouse? And why was he attacking the man?

Illegal poaching. Unlawful trade in wild species. One of Miles Cruise's favored businesses.

Had they found him? Ella turned to Brenner to voice her excitement. But she did not get a chance to speak.

The beast broke free. Then it charged, giving the man a mighty shove, slamming the latter against the window. It shattered.

The crowd gasped and scrambled back as the man tumbled headfirst, screaming, through a rainfall of glass.

Chapter 18

Ella and Brenner shoved through the gawkers, badges aloft. The body was draped over a huge snowdrift where plows had cleared the street. Shards of broken glass twinkled amid the grimy snow. The man released a faint groaning sound. He pushed himself up into crawling position, on hands and knees, then stayed there, gasping, shaking his head like a confused dog.

Ella let the cops and Brenner pass her and go to the victim. Instead, she looked up to the open window, hoping to see the animal that had done the damage. Clearly, they needed to clear out the crowd and call Fish and Wildlife if there was a wild bear on the loose.

A woolly behemoth stood in the window, peering down at them. Grey fur covered it from head to toe, but not bear fur. The fur had long gray tails hanging down from it.

Wolf pelts.

Wolf pelts, clumsily stitched together. And the face that peered out was neither that of a bear nor a wolf. It was a human face. Black brows, bristling beard, and a misshapen mouth, but definitely human.

The wolf man stared down at the street. No, not at the street, at his latest victim groaning amidst the snow, ice and shards of glass, with a couple of plainclothes men on their knees beside him. The beast inclined his head, then wordlessly turned and stalked away.

"Brenner!" She clutched the upper arm of his black jacket. "He's up there. He's in the window! The Wolf."

But Brenner pointed elsewhere, at the man on the ground.

"What?" she demanded.

"Look!" Brenner whispered fiercely.

She stared now, getting a good look at the man. His face was familiar. She'd been staring at it for the past day. Brown hair, well-groomed, former Marine, poacher, woman-beater and kidnapper.

Miles Cruise.

She blinked, stunned. The man they'd been looking for was on the ground in front of them, groaning, and rocking on snow and glass. Blood trickled from his broad forehead, his splayed hands.

Time slowed.

This was the criminal mastermind they sought? He looked more like a movie buffoon, the stooge nobody respected.

"Asshole," Miles was muttering. "Ungrateful asshole." One of the Marshals was checking him over, both for weapons and for injuries.

Her own thoughts whirled. Something had changed. Something big, and something they were missing.

The Wolf had been Miles' muscle...

So why had he just thrown the man out a window?

Unless they were missing something... Unless they'd made assumptions.

But what?

Now Brenner was cuffing Miles, the two plainclothes officers holding the latter upright. "My arm!" Cruise yelled. "Asshole--you're going to rip it off!"

The crowd had backed off and now began to disperse, couples and groups chattering about what they'd seen, individuals sending off films and selfies, all of them heading off to favored exhibits.

Ella cursed. "I'm going after the Wolf. Brenner, stay here!"

"Wait!" Brenner called, but Ella was already sprinting.

They were missing something... something big. But what? She had to know.

She tore through the open door of the warehouse and pounded across the concrete floor to where steel stairs led to an upper floor. She took the stairs three at a time.

She reached the top landing and paused to decide which way to turn down the long hallway. Everything was quiet, strangely quiet.

It was the sound of a forest when a predator was on the prowl.

She exhaled slowly, glancing down the gray, dingy corridor. Up here, the expo hadn't managed to extend its reach.

Now, her eyes raked the bare walls.

No sign of the Wolf. No sign of movement at all.

The expo below seemed like a distant thing now, a muffled dream. She shivered, breath coming in quick puffs. Her body still hadn't fully recovered from her time in the ocean, and the concrete walls seemed to hold in the winter chill. But she knew she was close to answers, she had to go on.

She unholstered her weapon, released the safety, and adopted a readiness stance. Gun in hand, knees flexed, she moved down the hall.

She'd always found an intrepid spirit when confronted with danger. Facing a feral man in this dark gray hall was just another challenge.

She moved quietly, a feral hunter herself, one foot in front of the other. Her hands were steady as stone, and the gun moved slowly, side to side as she swept her gaze from one doorway to the next. Her senses strained. She smelled old paint, the tang of rust, but not yet the aroma of wildlife. She listened, listened to the strange silence, knowing it was cover for a monster.

She stepped into the first room, pushing the door open until its handle hit the inside wall. It was entirely bare. No place to hide.

Same with the next room. And the next. Not even shelves for goods. Not even a stray pencil or clipboard for tracking stock.

The fourth room was small, a third of the size of the others, narrow and windowless. A large wooden table surrounded by chairs took up almost all the space. A half-burned pillar candle sat in the middle of the table on an old tin plate. Its flame flickered in the draft, casting eerie shadows across the walls.

At the far corner of the table, she spotted discarded sandwich wrappers and crumbs, and something else: a rusty key. She reached out and picked it up, feeling the cool metal beneath her fingers. It was unexpectedly heavy, as if it held secrets of its own.

She frowned. She had seen a key like this before, in Nome.

A key to a cage.

The cage imprisoning Kerry Lonegan, so the poachers could take her on a hunt, a hunt where they designated her as prey.

Ella pocketed the key and returned to the hall. As she neared the end of the corridor, she heard a faint noise, soft, almost like a whisper. She stilled, her heart thudding.

Five steps away, she could see another doorway, the last one in the corridor. She took a deep breath and began to move closer, her eyes scanning the darkness for any sign of her quarry.

She got to the door unscathed and reached for the handle. It jiggled.

Behind the door, a low growl sounded from the darkness. Her heart leapt into her throat as she realized that she was not alone.

Taking a deep breath, she raised her gun and pushed open the door.

It was jammed.

She yanked down on the handle all the way, thinking she hadn't felt it unlatch.

Still nothing happened, except that the growling sound faded.

Had it just been her imagination?

What had they missed?

She pressed her shoulder against the door, trying to shove it inwards, but it didn't budge. She tried again, this time slamming herself against the door. No deal.

She paused for a moment, trying to think of a way to get inside. But her mind remained blank.

The growl resumed again, much closer now. She could feel it vibrating through the walls.

Suddenly, an idea struck her. The door would not move, but maybe there was another way in. She pulled out her flashlight and began to scan the walls, searching for something...

Something...

There.

A vent.

She stared at the vent, made up her mind, and dashed back to the room with the table. There she grabbed the nearest chair by its sides and carried it to the hall.

She pushed the chair under the vent, then climbed onto it. She reached under the bulky coat, unclipping her utility knife from her belt.

Slowly and cautiously, she unscrewed the vent with the knife, avoiding unnecessary noise. The vent, unscrewed, wobbled dangerously. She held her breath as she pulled it free, hoping the sound wouldn't travel far. Her fingers touched grease. A second later the grate was sliding out of her hands.

As it fell to the floor, she twisted down and caught it again, preventing it from clattering against the hard surface. She tucked it between the chair and the wall, wedging it in place. Then she mounted the chair again, this time hoisting herself up to the air vent. She took a deep breath and squeezed through the small opening. Darkness enveloped her, but her eyes adjusted quickly.

She began feeling her way. It was dusty, and when she breathed in, she almost choked. It wasn't big enough for her to crawl on hands and knees, she had to pull herself along, breathing in short, sharp sniffs to minimize the particles going into her lungs. Her fingers and elbows scraped against the cold metal. When she got to an intersection, she squirmed around the corner, towards the locked room. Now she could see the vent cover.

She slid along until she could touch the cover, pushing it open. Her fingers tried to catch the metal before it fell.

Too late.

It clattered to the ground, echoing as it bounced. A roar greeted the cacophony.

Ella grimaced, waited for the noises to stop, then pushed out of the vent into the room beyond.

She found herself in a dimly lit storage area. The growling had stopped, but she could hear panting and snuffling noises coming from the other side of the room. She also heard scrapes against metal—the sounds of creatures in cages.

She pulled herself out of the vent to her waist, then gripped the edge of the duct and flipped herself over like a gymnast, down to the ground. Another roar. She pulled her gun and felt cold sweat breaking out on her forehead.

She stared at the large, shattered window. This was where the Wolf had flung Miles Cruise.

It still didn't make any sense.

Why had the Wolf turned on his boss?

Unless they had it backwards.

What if Cruise wasn't the boss?

What if the Wolf was?

What if this strange poacher, this sniper, wasn't the employee, but the employer? Cruise... a money man? A go-between?

It made sense.

But that left one question? Who the hell was the Wolf?

He was their real target if her hunch was right. So who was he?

All these thoughts pulsed through her mind while she scrutinized the room. Then, her eyes fell on the cage.

There, pressed against the wall, under a stack of compound bows and old, carbon arrows covered in dust, sat a cage about waist high.

She approached. The growling became a snarl.

She stared.

Two yellow eyes stared back at her.

A dog.

Ella's shoulders relaxed, and she began to laugh. Nothing more than a mangy dog. The poor creature looked ill-treated, with damp gray and white fur, mange, and drool trickling down its lips.

Now that she made no aggressive move, the dog loosed a small whimper. It circled the cage a couple of times, two steps across, two steps back. Through its fur, she could see its ribs.

No... no, not a dog.

What was it? A type of wolf?

Some creature ready for a hunt? She realized that around its rear leg, it wore a tight bracelet, with a little black box.

Not ready for a hunt. Ready to be hunted. Imprisoned under the very weapons the poachers would use to kill it.

And only now, as she glanced around, did she take in the rest of her surroundings.

There were two other cages, further back from the window, either side of the door that she had not been able to open. One of them was empty.

The other cage stood over seven feet tall and equally wide. It housed a fully grown grizzly, slumped against the wall. It was unable to lie down fully. As she saw it, it leaned forward, staring with wide, fiery eyes. Its chest heaved like a great set of bellows. Its teeth were bared, its claws curled into the metal bars. It roared in rage and frustration, and she flinched. She knew it would kill her if it could, in vengeance for its predicament. Slowly, she backed away.

It, too, wore a tracking device, in a collar around its neck.

A howl joined the bear's roar. Ella looked back at the emaciated wolf. Its lean body crashed against the side of its cage, its teeth and claws attacked the padlocked door.

The growling and snuffling noises escalated, as the anger of the two captives fed off each other. Finally, the grizzly rose almost to its full height, its head pressing against the top of the cage. It roared, shaking its head and slamming its paws against the metal bars. The canine whimpered into silence and slunk to the far side, submitting to the larger predator.

Assured of its dominance over at least one other pitiable creature, the bear resumed lounging against the wall, panting heavily.

Ella doubled back to the wolf cage, surveying the animal with a mix of curiosity and fear. Its hair was matted, but she could see the wolf's shape beneath the filth. Its hips were flexible, its muscles lean and powerful, and its paws thick and calloused. Despite its misery, she could see the potential for an unimaginable hunt...

There was evidence on the walls of other hunts.

The walls were adorned with faded photographs, depicting various scenes of chase and capture. There were pictures of lions, tigers, and even a massive anaconda coiled around a tree trunk. The size and ferocity of the animals were awe-inspiring, yet she felt pity as she saw them caged and impotent. She shuddered to think of the type of people who liked these rigged hunts.

As she examined the photographs, the significance of the empty cage finally hit her. It wasn't just an empty space; it was a missing piece in this twisted puzzle. The absence of a creature suggested that it had somehow escaped or been released. But what kind of creature was it?

She turned her attention back to the caged wolf. Now that it was used to her, its eyes pleaded for freedom. She couldn't deny the allure of setting it free, but she also had a responsibility to uncover the truth behind this place and put an end to its horrific practices.

Her eyes moved along the pictures hanging on the walls.

Trophies.

Trophies by a hunter who'd travelled the world.

The Wolf.

But where was he?

She approached the window, studying the jagged glass, looking for... something. Anything.

What had caused the Wolf to fling his partner through the glass?

Unless...

Had he known they were coming?

Or perhaps, more likely, he'd spotted them below and then reacted...

He'd used the one distraction he could.

Like any good hunter, he'd baited his prey with the proper bait.

Miles Cruise was now in custody.

But the real predator?

He was still on the loose.

Ella looked down, where Brenner knelt by their cuffed suspect. Despite being thrown through the window, Miles Cruise looked healthy enough. A few scrapes and cuts aside, he seemed in full possession of his outrage, on full display as he tongue-lashed Brenner.

At least he didn't mind chatting.

But what would he say?

Who was the Wolf?

How was Miles involved?

And what were they missing?

Chapter 19

Night had fallen over Juneau like a thick velvet curtain. The sky, a deep indigo, was void of stars, shrouded by the persistent ocean mist that clung to the city like a shadow. Ella Porter sat in the passenger seat of the police SUV, her gaze occasionally darting out the window before returning to the interior bathed in the soft green glow of the dashboard lights.

In the cocoon of the SUV, as it hummed through Juneau's nocturnal arteries, Ella Porter's gaze flickered to the rearview mirror where Miles Cruise's reflection brooded. The city lights threw his features into relief—every line on his forehead, every twist of discontent that marred his handsome face. He was the epitome of a man who had climbed the corporate ladder only to find it leaning against the wrong wall—a yuppie in appearance with his tailored suit now rumpled and tie askew, and the eyes of a spoiled toddler.

He didn't look much like the poacher they'd been warned about. He looked like a fraudster... A white-collar criminal. Not a rough-neck in the wilderness of the harshest state in the US.

And then she recalled Kerry Lonegan's fear at the mention of this man's name, the scars on her arms, the way she had run away to Alaska with an unknown woman to get away from Cruise. Cruise's corporate style was a façade, a cover for the brute underneath.

"Nice night for a drive, isn't it?" she ventured casually.

He glared at her, then turned his face to his window.

Ella took her time, counting her heartbeats. Each beat seemed to sync with the flash of passing streetlights. She studied him again in the mirror. His jaw was clenched, a muscle twitching in his cheek. The man's silk and cashmere coat screamed Wall Street (at least it had before he was pitched out a window onto a dirty snowdrift), yet there he was, sitting in the back of an Alaskan police vehicle looking as out of place as a wolf in sheep's clothing—or was it the other way around?

"Juneau can be lovely this time of year," she continued, embodying a perky tour guide, hoping to elicit more than silent animosity. "That is, if you're not too busy getting acquainted with storefront windows."

The joke fell flat, absorbed by the hum of the engine and Brenner's steady hands on the wheel.

Miles shifted, crossing his arms. His sullen demeanor was a lockbox, but Ella was patient. She could find her way around locks.

"Comfortable back there?" she pressed, refusing to let the quiet take hold again.

"Ecstatic," he finally muttered, the word dripping with sarcasm and something else—fear, perhaps?

"Relax," she said, her tone softer now. "We just want to get to the bottom of this. And you're going to help us, aren't you?"

The SUV hit a pothole, jouncing them all. Brenner muttered an apology, but Ella barely heard him. Her attention was riveted on the man behind her, watching as his Adam's apple bobbed with a hard swallow.

"Sure, Agent Porter," he replied after a heavy pause. "I'll help. But sometimes... sometimes the bottom is deeper than you think."

"Then we better start digging," she responded, her voice steel.

He'd mentioned a few times now his willingness to help, but he'd yet to volunteer anything.

He seemed like someone trying to keep his options open.

The night dropped over Juneau like a shroud, wrapping itself around streetlamps and spilling into alleyways. Inside the police SUV, the darkness was kept at bay by the glow of instrument panels and the soft overhead light that cast an interrogation-room ambiance over the backseat.

"Mr. Cruise," Ella began, her words clipped as she twisted to face him more fully from the passenger seat. "Why don't we start with something easy?"

"Sure thing, sugar. You can drop me off right here."

She ignored the jibe, "Care to explain how you ended up being thrown through a window tonight?" She could see his silhouette stiffen against the fabric of the car seat, his shadowed profile framed by the passing lights.

The muscle in Miles Cruise's cheek flicked again. He stared straight ahead, his eyes fixed on some distant point beyond the windshield. "I don't see how that's any of your business, Agent Porter."

"Must've been some disagreement," she mused, her fingers tapping a silent code of impatience against her thigh.

"Disagreements happen in business." Miles's voice was flat, dismissive, but that tic in his cheek again betrayed his cool exterior. Ella took note of the white-knuckled grip he had on the seatbelt, the slight narrowing of his eyes.

"Right. But not everyone ends a disagreement with a trip through plate glass."

He gave no response, turning his head slightly to gaze out of the tinted window as if willing himself to disappear into the

Alaskan night. Ella's eyebrows knit together in frustration, but her voice remained calm.

"Talk to me, Miles," she prodded, softening her voice to a persuasive murmur. "Help us understand."

More silence. Ella knew this dance well—the push and pull of interrogation—and she settled into her seat, ready for the long haul. In the quiet, her mind whirred, shuffling pieces of the puzzle, waiting for another bit of information to link them together. She was certain that Miles Cruise held the missing piece.

Brenner navigated the icy streets without comment. He had tried to raise a response from Cruise while Ella was in the warehouse. Miles had offered nothing other than cursing complaints about his unjust situation.

"Let's talk about the Wolf," Ella broke the silence abruptly. “Your good friend.” The words held accusation.

In the rearview mirror, she caught Miles Cruise's reaction. His face blanched at the mention of the nickname. He looked like a man who had just seen a ghost—or rather, feared one was lurking around the corner, ready to pounce.

"Who?" Miles managed, his voice a croak, feigning ignorance.

"Come on, Miles. You know exactly who I'm talking about," Ella chided, firm but not unkind. “He's the guy who shoved you through that window. The one who watches over *your* illegal animals in *your* warehouse." It wasn't a question of if he knew the Wolf; it was how deep he was in with him.

Miles fidgeted, his hands clenching and unclenching. "I don't—I don't know what you're talking about."

Ella's sharp blue gaze saw his discomfort. His whole body pulsated, even his breath quivered. Fear had wrapped its cold fingers around Miles Cruise, the same revulsion that Petrov had exhibited.

"Your poker face needs work," she observed dryly. "You look like someone just walked over your grave."

"Is that supposed to scare me into talking?" he shot back, but without full conviction.

"Scaring you isn't my goal," Ella replied, shifting tactics. "Protection is. But I can't help if you won't be honest with me."

"Protection?" Miles scoffed, but the word seemed to echo in the cramped space of the vehicle, resonating with a possibility he hadn't considered.

"From the Wolf, yes," Ella confirmed. Her eyes never wavered from his reflection, every subtle change in his expression. "But you need to talk to me, Miles. What are you afraid of?"

Miles swallowed hard, his gaze darting away from hers. "You think you can protect anyone from... from something like that?

Sometimes you can use him. He makes problems go away, while having fun. But you can never control him. And no one can stop him."

"Let me try," Ella challenged. She leaned in slightly, closing the distance, even if only symbolically. "Start by telling me how you're involved."

Silence filled the SUV once more, but it was different now—charged not with defiance, but with the electricity of desperation. Miles's eyes met hers again in the mirror, and for a fleeting moment, she saw a plea for help.

"Can't," he whispered.

"Can't? Or won't?" Ella's question was like a hammer to glass. She sensed the barrier between them fracturing, giving way under the weight of his dread. "Miles, whatever it is, it's clear you're in over your head." It was hard for her to keep her voice compassionate, now that she understood that Cruise had bought the Wolf's enforcement skills by monetizing the latter's hunger for prey. If her understanding was correct, they were both monsters.

Cruise looked away again, his face a canvas of conflict. Ella watched as he wrestled with himself, with the danger of speaking and the peril of remaining silent.

"Talk to me," she urged once more, her voice a lifeline thrown across the chasm of his fear. "Before it's too late."

She still didn't know the full extent of Cruise's role in all of this. He was a prime suspect in a murder investigation. The poaching operation was credited to him. He was the one making money off animals in cages... And what about the women? Had that been his idea too? And what others?

"Who is the Wolf, Miles?" Ella pressed again, her voice steady despite the pounding of her heart. "What got you involved with him? What does he want with you?"

Miles' lips trembled as if he were about to speak, but no words issued from his mouth. Instead, his eyes darted around the interior of the vehicle like those of his caged animals, searching for escape. She could almost hear his thoughts scattering in panic, clawing for a way out that didn't exist.

She needed to find some in. Some way to crack him.

"Is it money? Power?" she continued, probing the edges of his terror. "Or is it something personal?"

He shuddered, and his Adam's apple bobbed as he swallowed hard. His fingers knotted together, knuckles whitening from the strain. "You don't know what you're asking," he finally managed, the pitch of his voice rising.

"Help me understand, then." Ella's gaze never wavered.

Suddenly, Miles jerked forward. He scrambled for the door handle with his cuffed hands, his movements erratic and wild.

He yanked at it and the lock—the lock that only the police driver should have been able to control—clicked open. The car door swung open, only for the wind to slam shut again.

"Stop the car!" he yelled, voice cracking on the final word. His hand fumbled with the seat belt, releasing it with a sharp click.

"Damn it, Miles, sit down!" Ella snapped. "Stop, Miles! Stop!"

His cuffs were still tight on his wrists, but he kept prying at the door handle. It should've been locked. There should have been no way for him to open it from the inside.

Unless someone had tampered with it. Unless someone had set them up.

Then, without warning, as if responding to some unseen trigger, Miles Cruise flung the door open and hurled himself out into the bitter cold. A gasp escaped Ella's lips, the world slowing to a crawl as she watched him tumble onto the hard-packed snow. He bounced once, violently, before rolling to his knees, finding his feet and sprinting away.

Ella's heart thrashed against her ribs as she watched Cruise stumble up the slope.

How could this happen? And why the hell was Brenner keeping the car moving?

"Stop the car! Brenner, stop the damn car!"

Brenner wrenched the wheel to the right. The SUV yawed precipitously, careening off the highway. The rubber tire treads screeched in protest, and Ella's body lurched against the constraints of her seatbelt. A plume of snow burst upwards like a geyser against the side windows as they skidded to an ungraceful halt, half-buried at the roadside.

"Go, go, go!" she shouted, already throwing her door open before the vehicle had fully rocked to a stop. Brenner was hot on her heels, his own door slamming shut behind him. She noticed he'd had the presence of mind to slap the emergency lights on before exiting. Now they flashed on and off, on and off, illuminating the roadside as jerkily as if they watched an old, broken reel-to-reel film.

They left the car as they slogged up the incline. If the moon had risen, they could not see it because of the mountain peak to the east. A few stars twinkled in between the scudding clouds. They turned on their flashlights, panning illumination across the slope. Ahead, Miles' figure was a blurred shadow sprinting up toward the tree line, but he left deep footprints in his wake. His arms propelled him forward, while his breath gusted out in ragged clouds.

"Damn it, Miles!" Ella cried out. She took off after him, her boots sinking in the snow. It came up almost to her knees and she had to pull hard to lift her legs high enough for the next step. She slogged to the right, aiming for Cruise's tracks. When she got to them, she followed the trail he had blazed, using his path to her advantage.

Brenner grunted affirmatively beside her. His breathing was easy still, he was in great condition, but the limp made his steps uneven. He was built like a man who could wrestle the world into submission, but speed was no longer his best weapon, his injury a reminder that battle had enduring consequences.

"Stop, Miles! There's nowhere to run!" she yelled, though she knew it was futile. Miles was beyond reason, propelled by emotion alone.

"Keep on him!" Brenner's affirmation spurred her to pump her legs faster.

She focused solely on the fleeing figure ahead. She could almost feel the pulse of his fear, a desperate cadence that matched her own relentless drive. The chase was everything—the icy bite of the wind against her face, the snow beneath her feet, the distant echo of Brenner's now labored breathing.

Ella's boots crunched rhythmically through the snow, a percussive counterpoint. Her breath trailed behind her like spectral echoes. A fox's paw prints, light on the snow's surface, crossed the deeper human tracks she followed. She kept up her pace, gaining on Cruise, every stride bringing her closer.

And then, her foot glanced the edge of a rock under the snow. Scrambling for balance, she had to look around to correct her bearings. She saw the snow, miles and miles of it, and the black hulk of the mountain looming ahead. There were no houses, no lights, except far behind and below her where Juneau glowed on the horizon. Looking into that vast darkness, a new thought struck her with the force of a physical blow. The wilderness around them seemed too open, too exposed. Every instinct, honed by years of fieldwork, screamed that something was off.

They were being baited, she was sure of it.

And yet, she couldn't stop—wouldn't stop—until she had Miles. She would not let this killer get away, however mealy-mouthed and pathetic he might be. Even if the effort cost her. She took off again, slogging forward, her boots eating away at his tracks.

She risked a glance over her shoulder; Brenner had fallen behind, his silhouette staggering slightly under the weight of his injury.

"Damn leg," she heard him curse. He was massaging his thigh, trying to increase speed.

She wanted to wait for him, needed his backup, but Miles' figure was growing smaller, getting further away with every second she hesitated. He was halfway to the tree line. She pushed forward alone.

As she crested a fold in the rise, her heart drummed an erratic rhythm, and not just from the chase. It struck her again, how exposed they were. The snowy slope offered nowhere to hide, no shadows in which to cloak their approach. A few barren trees stood like skeletal lookouts, providing no cover, and the rolling wilderness stretched all across the ridgeline.

"Christ, Brenner," she muttered under her breath, "there's nothing out here. No cover. It's like he led us into the open on purpose."

Now each step felt like a march into a snare, carefully laid so that she could not see it. Her hands tightened around the grip of her weapon, its cold metal a solid reassurance amidst the swirling doubts.

Miles seemed to risk a glance back, she could not tell for sure, her flashlight bobbed with each step. For a heartbeat, she had the feeling that their gazes locked, a silent battle of wills before he turned away, pushing himself forward and up.

"Got you," Ella whispered to herself, sensing the shift, the momentary weakness in his resolve. She could feel the distance closing between them, her own body reaching its limits. Pain seared the muscles of her legs as she willed herself to increase speed, kicking up snow with every toilsome step.

"Enough, Miles!" she shouted. "Let this end now!"

His body twisted, his pace faltering ever so slightly. For a second, Ella thought she saw him stumble, but he regained his footing and speed.

Her lungs burned with exertion, each inhale sharp and cold, yet training kept her going, her focus unwavering.

The gap lessened—ten yards...five... Ella's hand reached out to grab Miles' jacket and haul him to the ground.

The sharp crack of a gunshot tore through the silence. Ella's outstretched hand caught nothing but air because the force of the shot threw Miles Cruise forward. Ella's eyes, wide with shock, could only watch as his body crumpled into the snow.

"Down!" she instinctively screamed, but her warning was too late for Miles.

He lay motionless, his face turned sideways as though on a pillow, his lips moving in soundless speech. The glare of her flashlight showed the hole in his chest, and the blood staining the pristine white snow around him. The contrast was jarring, the red so vivid against the monochrome landscape that it seemed almost surreal.

The trap had sprung, but not for her.

Chapter 20

"Who—" Ella's voice hitched in her throat, her mind scrambled to make sense of it all. Only one thing was clear: there was a killer on the mountain.

She turned off her flashlight and veered away from Miles. When a deep pocket of snow tripped her up, she pushed to the side and rolled across the surface.

"Cover!" she shouted, though surely Brenner was already aware, hobbling through the snow to find anything that could serve as protection. But she could not see him. He had turned his flashlight off too. Her ears strained and she thought she could hear his breathing, breathing almost as familiar to her as her own.

Now cloaked by darkness, she began edging back towards Cruise. She kept low in the snow, her heart pounding in tandem with the throb of her overworked muscles. She needed to confirm the kill, the agent in her overriding fear of personal danger.

"Stay down, check your angles," she reminded herself.

Above her, a puff of wind parted the clouds like a theatre curtain, revealing the splendor of the Milky Way. The starlight also revealed the outline of Cruise's body. She only hoped the hidden man with the rifle could not see her.

Kneeling beside Miles, she saw the light fading from his eyes, his breaths bubbling with scarlet froth. "Hang on," she said, more reflex than reassurance. "Help is coming." But even as she spoke, she knew it was a lie. The blood was pooling too quickly, the wound gaping and fatal. His breathing stopped.

"Damn it," she cursed under her breath. They needed answers from him, and all they had now was a body and more questions. "Cover! We need—"

Her words ended in a gasp, as arms wrapped around Ella's waist, dragging her down with the force of a battering ram. Snow erupted around them as they tumbled to the ground, a soft white blanket turning into a cold shield. She twisted to fight free, then saw the familiar curve of Brenner's cheek next to her.

"Down!" His voice was a gruff whisper, a command born from years of combat.

"Who is it?" Ella gasped. There was no time to be gentle; this was survival.

"Can't see, but they're close," Brenner replied. He raised his head, eyes scanning the tree line beyond the clearing. The weight of his body pinned her to the ground. "Stay down." He scouted the terrain with his gaze. "Listen to me, Ella," Brenner said close to her ear, his breath warm against her cold cheek. "When I give the word, we move fast. Back to the SUV."

"Got it." She readied herself, her mind calculating tactics and escape routes.

"Wait for my mark..."

The silence lengthened. Ella's pulse throbbed in her ears, her body coiled tight, ready to spring.

"Go!"

Just then, the world seemed to freeze as the ominous crack of another gunshot ripped through the stillness. This time, the shot sounded closer than the last time.

Snow erupted at the ground beneath her feet. She careened sideways, grabbing Brenner's arm. The two of them stumbled away from Miles Cruise's corpse, over the ridge and back down into the hollow of the slope. They found their old tracks, trampling through the powder as they sprinted towards the SUV.

The Wolf. It had to be.

The man behind all of this. They'd thought Miles Cruise was the main threat, the poacher...

But Cruise's death proved them wrong. Something else was going on here.

As they ran, the landscape became a blur of white, the cold stinging their exposed skin. Brenner began to slow, his limp dragging him sideways.

The crack of another gunshot echoed through the air. They kept going, knowing that to stop would make them easier targets.

"Hang on, Brenner," Ella panted, her words ragged. "We're almost there."

He grunted in response and pushed himself harder.

As they drew closer to the SUV, she could see the driver's side door hanging open. The emergency lights no longer flashed. The engine slept.

"Quick, check the back," she instructed Brenner, drawing her gun as she approached. The front seats were empty. “Clear!”

“Clear here too,” Brenner called from the back. He clambered in beside her, his breathing labored.

Ella revved the engine, the cold flaying her fingers as she gripped the steering wheel. The world was a blur as she gunned the engine. It faltered and died.

"Shit," she said. "He's hit the engine. We're not moving."

Another gunshot. A second later, Ella heard something ping the front hood. “Shit!”

Brenner was already crawling over the passenger seat into the back. "Cover me!" he yelled. Ella maneuvered herself across the center console into the passenger seat to jam her weapon out the window, trying to track the direction of the gunshots. She fired off a burst, each shot echoing loudly in the confined space.

She watched as Brenner snatched at the rifle case in the back portion of the SUV. She winced as the glass window next to him exploded, and shards scattered across Brenner's shoulders. He cursed and ducked. After a second, he grabbed at the case again, dragging it into the back seat on top of himself where he lay, his shoulders pressed against the faux leather material. He fumbled with the clasps, trying to withdraw his rifle.

He inhaled deeply. Now his fingers moved with deft precision, his practiced skill clearly overcoming anxiety. Ella kept scanning the ridgeline, looking for any sign of the sniper. Where was he?

But in the cold, amid the snow, with the clouds moving across the sky, it all looked the same, a vast sea of white stretching up the mountain.

Brenner now had his rifle out of the case. Moving rapidly, he assembled the scope and the stand. He kept low, lying back on the seat, pulling the parts out of the case by feel.

A lull settled over the mountain slope.

The rifle was a familiar companion to Brenner, and he treated it as such, as if it were an extension of himself. Each part fitted precisely into place. The clicks of pieces slotting together, and the scratch of screws tightening the fit marked his progress despite the confined space of the SUV.

The world outside was a frosty wasteland, the horizon stretched as far as the eye could see. The gunfire had stopped for now, but Ella knew it wouldn't be long before the sniper resumed his hunt. It was his passion.

Every few seconds, an icy breeze blew through the open door and shattered window. Sometimes it carried the distant howls of wolves. Did they know they had a human counterpart? Did they fear him too, like the caged wolf back in the Juneau warehouse?

Ella's eyes never left the ridgeline. Their survival depended on her watchfulness.

Finally, with a soft click, Brenner finished assembling the rifle. He tested the scope, ensuring that it was functioning properly.

"You good?" she asked.

Brenner gave a quick nod. "You see him?"

She hesitated, still scanning the ridgeline. "No... No, but he's west. Shots are coming east."

Brenner nodded, frowned as he gauged the wind by the flapping tag above the seatbelt.

"He's not moving," Brenner whispered. "I don't see him."

He kept peering through the scope, scanning the ridge.

"He's an expert hunter," Ella said, also keeping low. "We need to draw him out."

"How?"

"I have an idea, but you're not going to like it."

"Ella," he said sharply.

But she waved a hand over her shoulder. "See the snowbank? Where we skidded off the road? I can race to it."

"Snow's not going to give you any cover."

"But it will obscure his line of sight."

"No. Don't be silly."

"We can't stay here," she retorted. "It's too cold. We'll freeze. Engine's dead."

"We've got warmers in the back."

"Think it's safer to get those?"

Brenner huffed in frustration.

Ella's hand was on the door handle before Brenner could protest further. They were sitting ducks. For all she knew, the sniper was moving to a new location, finding a more lethal angle.

"Ready?" she pressed.

"Ella!" he warned.

She flipped her blue hood up, hiding her pale hair, and charged out of the vehicle.

Chapter 21

The world seemed to narrow down to the pounding of her heart and the icy air filling her lungs. Flurries started to dance through the air, blowing down the mountain slope and across the road. She propelled herself forward, boots crunching on the ice on the shoulder as she zigzagged the 30 yards across the terrain to where their SUV first left the road. Her blue gaze scanned every shadow, every anomaly that could betray the sniper's position.

"Come on, show yourself," she muttered, each breath forming a cloud that dissipated quickly in the frigid air. She could feel the sniper's eyes on her, his hunger a tangible weight against her skin.

But to her surprise, no gunshots resounded.

She dived behind a clump of churned snow and mud. If he got her in his sights—no, when he did—the slightest twitch of his finger would mean a bullet with her name etched into its leaden heart.

"Where are you?" she breathed, knowing full well the sniper wouldn't answer. Her own voice sounded alien in the hushed landscape. Every second lengthened, an eternity wrapped in cotton wool silence.

Her mind raced—calculating distances, assessing angles, replaying every piece of intel they had on the shooter.

What did they really know about the Wolf?

Nothing.

Only that he invoked fear in everyone who encountered him.

Ella's chest heaved. She darted to a new position, a spray of snow marking her path. No crack of a rifle followed. The silence was suffocating, the absence of sound more alarming than the report of gunfire.

"Anything?" she asked through clenched teeth, subvocalizing into the comm unit nestled snugly in her ear.

"Negative," Brenner's voice dripped disapproval. "No movement on the ridge."

"Keep watching," she urged, hoping her voice didn't betray the frustration seething inside. She crouched low, scanning the horizon herself. Why wasn't he taking the shot? Ella's mind churned with possibilities.

He knows we're baiting him.

"Damn it," she muttered under her breath, feeling the sting of failure nip at her nerves. He was toying with them, playing on their expectations, and turning their plan against them. It dawned on her that every move she made might be exactly what he anticipated.

"Brenner." Her words throbbed with frustration. "He's onto us. He knows we're trying to flush him out."

"Roger that." There was a rustle from Brenner's end, the faintest whisper of movement as he shifted his weight. "Don't give him any patterns to work with."

"Patterns..." Ella's gaze flicked across the landscape. They needed to be unpredictable, chaotic even. Something to throw off the sniper's anticipation. She took a deep breath and expelled it slowly, allowing the cold to seep into her lungs—steel for her resolve that wavered ever so slightly.

"Copy," she confirmed, her tone icy as the ground.

She remained crouched by the snowy barrier, thinking. What was she missing?

Something obvious...

But what?

She shivered, hunching in her too big coat.

What pattern...

She hesitated, then pulled out her phone.

"What are you doing?" Brenner's voice crackled in her ear.

"Changing the pattern," she whispered back.

She tugged off a glove to sign into the phone and start navigating. The device connected to a SAT flash drive which provided internet even in harsh conditions. The cold nipped her fingertips as she punched links.

She couldn't go long without gloves, but she needed something to scramble the pattern. To reveal who this Wolf really was.

How was he connected to Miles Cruise? Why had he turned on the man?

Was he employer or employee? Mastermind or muscle? They had no proper name for the Wolf. And there'd been no mention of it in Miles' file. They had missed something.

She glanced across the cold white, up the slope, past the ridgeline, to where she knew Miles' corpse lay in the snow. Her phone displayed the dead man's information. Known associates... She began scanning the names.

She scrolled to each name, clicked the link to photos and information, and scrolled on. Her fingertips had begun to sting, the cold a thousand tiny needles. The first few contacts were acquaintances, business partners, and close friends. None of them matched the description of the Wolf. A large man... she'd glimpsed him herself. An enormous man, a sniper, wearing wolf pelts. A poacher by trade, and a long-distance shooter.

These bankers and lawyers...

None of them fit the bill.

She kept scanning through, her tongue tucked inside of her cheek. Curled on the ground in the shelter of the snowbank, absorbed in her task, she barely felt the cold except in her fingers, now starting to go numb.

She paused, to glove her cold hand and navigate with the other. She could hear Brenner breathing softly in the radio receiver. She knew he continued to survey the ridgeline from his foxhole in the wheel wells of the back seat.

And then she had an idea...

Known associates were automatically filtered by those still livi ng...

But what if...

She tapped the link for deceased associates. Again, the list seemed populated by unlikely candidates.

But the last name caught her attention: Samantha Cruise.

A sister.

Samantha Cruise had died three years ago.

Ella frowned. She clicked the link. Samantha Cruise, according to a death certificate, had died almost exactly three years ago. Some news articles found on the internet told the story in harrowing detail.

Samantha Cruise had been killed by her own husband. Ella frowned, skimming the article, her breath coming in quick puffs. She was all too aware of a sniper out there, somewhere, watching.

She shifted a bit, her back still pressed to the cold snowdrift.

"Come on," she whispered to herself.

Miles Cruise's sister had been killed by a man named Jason St. Pierre. According to the article, St. Pierre had found his wife cheating on him. He'd kidnapped her, dragged her out into the wilderness on the slopes of Mount Rainier...

Where the two of them jumped off the side of an icy cliff.

Ella doubted that Samantha had jumped willingly.

She stared at the article now, nibbling on the corner of her lip. Only Samantha's body had been found...

She clicked Jason's name.

A photo appeared.

A picture of a grizzled man with scarred features... A massive man. Nearly six foot five and three hundred pounds.

And according to the article, he'd trained as a sniper for a SWAT team in Seattle.

"Shit," she whispered softly. She now fully understood the interest of the Seattle FBI, and why they had wanted her on this "poaching" case.

"What is it?" Brenner's voice crackled through her earpiece.

"I think I know who's hunting us."

"Who?"

"His name is Jason St. Pierre. He killed his wife. Staged his own death."

"You sure it's him?"

"No. But it fits... He was a SWAT sniper. His wife two-timed him. He figured it out and dealt with her."

"How?"

"He killed her on a mountain cliff." She paused. "Get this, she was Miles's sister."

"Wait? What? So Cruise was employing the man who killed his sister?"

"Looks... looks like maybe it was the other way around. St. Pierre came from money. A hunter by trade. His great grandfather owned a trapping empire across the Yukon."

"Shit. So... he killed his wife then hired his brother-in-law... to what?"

Ella was shaking her head. "We'd have to go through the finan cials... but I bet he's hunting for fun. Those women we found? I bet Miles procured them."

"So he's repeating the murder of his wife? Again and again..."

"Not to mention the wildlife he's going after. And Cruise mentioned others. Rival criminals?"

Brenner cleared his throat hesitantly. "It's... I mean, we all have to eat."

"I'm not saying anything about that," she said quickly, knowing that Brenner was an avid hunter in his spare time. "But poaching is a different game. And hunting women?"

"Right. So... we know who this sicko is. How do we draw him out?"

Ella considered this for a moment. "He's ex-SWAT," she said slowly. "He's likely got comms... Alright. I have an idea."

"Ella," Brenner said, a note of warning in his voice.

"No, really. This should work." And then she reached for her radio.

Chapter 22

Ella crouched behind her snowy barricade. She still held the radio tightly in her hand, wondering if she was making the right choice.

"Damn it," she muttered to herself, her breath visible in the frigid air. The radio crackled in her hand, a lifeline to a world that felt miles away from this frozen hellscape. "Brenner, you still with me?"

"Still here," came the terse reply, static wobbling his voice. "I don't think this is a good idea."

"Stay put, keep your head down." She clutched the radio tighter, moving only her eyes as she scanned her environment.

St. Pierre was out there—somewhere—his motives colder than the Alaskan winter. The man was a predator, his sights set on them now. Ella knew what he was capable of; she had seen it firsthand. Yet, giving him a name, learning something about his past, gave her something to work with, something that made him smaller in her eyes: a monstrous human, not an alien predator.

A faint rustling sound broke her focus. Ella froze, every muscle tensed. Could be the wind, she thought, or a death sentence disguised as the wilderness. Her finger hovered over the trigger guard, the metal biting into her skin.

Ella crouched, peering over the snow drift. Ice crystals bit at her cheeks. The radio in her gloved hand hummed softly with static. Frost had begun to rime it, except where the battery emitted warmth.

She tuned the radio to an open channel, hoping her guess about St. Pierre and comms was correct.

"St. Pierre," she hissed into the handset. "You think you're hunting us? Guess again."

She was almost certain he'd be listening. He'd tracked them somehow, he'd followed them. This had all been part of his hunt. He'd used his brother-in-law as bait.

Ella grimaced. She sure hoped she knew what she was doing.

"Your wife sends her regards, by the way," she mocked. "Seems she's been warming other beds during your disappearing act."

Ella shifted, seeking the SUV's ghostly outline. St. Pierre could be lining up a shot right now, his scope a cyclopean eye searching for her heat signature. The fingers of her free hand curled around the Glock tucked in her belt, the cold metal a grim comfort.

"Must sting, knowing you faked your death for nothing. You're not just a murderer, St. Pierre, but a cuckold too. How's that for a double whammy?" She wanted anger, wanted him rattled and making mistakes.

The silence stretched, taut as a wire. Ella waited, still on the outside, inside plotting paths through the snow, strategies to stay alive. Every shadow looked like a rifle barrel, every whisper of wind a bullet.

"Come out, come out, wherever you are," she taunted, prodding the beast. She knew the caged grizzly would have lashed out at the tactic. She hoped it would work with St. Pierre. She wanted to goad him into making a mistake that would reveal his position.

Ella's breath misted in the frigid air. She kept her voice steady. "You know what's worse than being dead, St. Pierre? Being a pawn in your own sick game. How many did Miles bring to you, huh? Innocent women thinking they'd found adventure in Alaska, only to become prey."

"Truth hurts, doesn't it?" Ella pressed the transmit button, ensuring St. Pierre heard every word. "They were people, not just targets for your twisted hunts."

Only static answered her, but she knew he was out there, listening, smoldering.

She glanced at the SUV, its engine silent and still. Brenner was inside, his presence both a comfort and a concern. Ella switched channels.

"Status, Brenner?" she whispered.

"Blown engine, we're sitting ducks here," Brenner's frustration was evident even through the static. "Any movement?"

"Nothing yet." Her eyes scanned the terrain, searching for the telltale glint of a scope. "Stay low, keep watch."

There was a pause, then, "Be careful, El."

"Likewise," she responded. Brenner was more than a partner; he was the one person she trusted without question.

She switched radio frequencies again. "How is it?" she jeered. "Being a cuckold, I mean? Hardly a man. Half a man, really..." Ella was usually polite. But now she needed to make her words sting.

And they did.

A gunshot blast split the dark. Ella flinched as she watched the SUV's hatch window crack, a spider-web of destruction weaving across the glass.

"Sniper!" Brenner's voice jagged in her earpiece. "South ridge, third pine to the left."

"Copy." She didn't acknowledge the cold seeping through her gloves, the snow that clung to her like a shroud.

"Can you get to him?" That was the crucial question.

"Only one way to find out." Ella shifted, muscles ready beneath layers of winter gear. She crept forward, each movement deliberate, blending with the dark night. Away from the car, she had a better chance of moving unseen.

"Keep your head down," Brenner warned, his words echoing her own plan.

Eyes locked on her target, she crawled forward. Snow filtered into her boots and her collar, stinging, a reminder she was very much alive.

"Movement, your six!" The urgency in Brenner's tone spiked her pulse.

Ella pressed flat, the snow a cold kiss against her cheek.

"Distraction in three," Brenner informed her. Through her radio she could hear him move.

"Got it." Ella tensed, prepared to spring, her fingers tightening around the grip of her gun. This was the dance they knew so well, life and death played out on a stage of snow and silence.

"Two."

"Ready."

"One."

The noise of Brenner's shot was her signal. Ella slithered, a serpent in the snow. Her spread-out body weight and small stature kept her from sinking into the drifts. The looming mountain shadowed her progress, and the swish of her movements was nothing more than whispers of the wind. With each inch gained, she drew closer to the hunter who had become the hunted.

Another shot rang out from the car behind her, down on the road. Somewhere between heartbeats, Ella counted the seconds, measuring time by Brenner's steady rhythm. This time, return fire came, a bullet singing past Brenner's hidden position, embedding itself into the frozen earth with a muted thud.

"Missed," Brenner muttered, relieved.

But Ella had gotten what she needed. She had seen the spark of the bullet as it exited St. Pierre's barrel, the only light on the mountain side. Now she knew where he was.

Her eyes fixed on the spot. Once they adjusted, she could see the outline of his dark form on the snow, a blot on the landscape. She wondered if he could see her too and hoped, that Brenner's gun consumed St. Pierre's attention. She thought of St. Pierre's size, how he'd loom over her if he stood. But so what? She had her own skills. She crawled forward some more, heading straight for the wolf man.

"Keep him busy," she whispered to Brenner, barely audible even to her own ears. Any louder and St. Pierre would hear. The open snow carried sound whenever the wind paused.

"Doing my best," Brenner replied. As if to prove it, another shot from the car split the night.

Her fingers brushed against new tracks, deep tracks made by large human boots. There was something icy and hard splotching the snow between them. She realized it was blood, frozen atop the snow. St. Pierre had come through here, crossing the snow to his current position. And he was wounded.

"Can't get a clean shot," Brenner breathed tersely.

"Doesn't matter," Ella thought, her gaze never wavering from the massive shape ahead. She could see that St. Pierre, too, lay in the snow, rifle scope aimed at a target on the road below. At Brenner.

As she edged nearer, the magnitude of St. Pierre's frame became clear. Even lying down, he seemed to command the land around him, his body a fortress under the wolfskins. She knew that underneath his winter gear he itched for battle, ready for a fight or flight that wouldn't come—not if she had anything to say about it.

St. Pierre moved slightly, angling for a better shot. Ella stiffened, her heart pounding so furiously she thought he might hear it. In that moment, she saw the broad expanse of his back, a target she couldn't miss.

Silently, she rose to her feet, pulling out her Glock with numb but steady fingers. She stood mere feet behind St. Pierre, whose massive silhouette lay against the snow like some dormant behemoth. Past him, she could see the glow of lights from Juneau at the edge of the horizon.

"St. Pierre," Ella's command echoed across the snow. "Don't move." Her gun aimed squarely at the back of his head.

The giant braced, a low growl escaping him. His hand hovered over his rifle, inches away from sealing Brenner's fate.

"Drop the weapon!" she directed, sharp as a drill sergeant, despite her hammering pulse.

St. Pierre didn't speak, but chuckled, a rumble as dark as the night. He kept the gun raised, his eye to the scope. It was almost as if he didn't care that she was there or fear what she threatened.

Ella took a step forward, tightening her aim.

"Try it, and you're dead before you can squeeze that trigger," she spat, her eyes never leaving the broad line of his shoulders.

Now St. Pierre twisted to look at her. She saw dark eyes under thick brows, a mouth twisted with scar tissue, skin creased by the outdoors, framed by a hood of pelts matted here and there with some dark substance. Blood, she thought. Blood from his kills. His dark gaze fixated on her for barely a second, assessing the menace, then he returned his attention to his scope as though she didn't exist.

The vast Alaskan wilderness seemed to hold its breath, waiting for what came next.

"Move away from the rifle," she enunciated, each word a spike of ice.

St. Pierre's laugh was a low rumble. He shifted slightly, testing her resolve.

Ella was surprised, but her hand remained steady. She could see the outline of his fingers tightening on the trigger of his rifle.

Was Brenner in his sights?

Panic clawed at her chest at the thought of Brenner catching a bullet. And her standing there, doing nothing.

The standoff stretched on, seconds piling upon seconds. St. Pierre leaned toward his weapon.

"Stop!" she barked, tightening her grip on the gun, her finger over the trigger. Her jaw clenched. She could feel him calculating, his mind working through scenarios where he came out on top.

"Back. Away. Now." Her voice left no room for negotiation, even as anxiety roiled her insides.

His answer was another rumbled laugh. His hand moved, deliberate and slow, closing around his rifle stock. Ella's breath hitched, her entire focus narrowing down to that one motion.

The click of St. Pierre's trigger was like the tick of a death clock in the icy Juneau air. Ella could almost see the bullet carving its deadly path toward Brenner. Her heart clenched at the thought.

"Dammit, no!" she spat through clenched teeth.

Her next move was instinct, honed by years of training and decades of nightmares. Her finger responded, pulling the Glock trigger even before her mind could analyze St. Pierre's own finger pressure on his rifle. The sharp report of her gun echoed across the mountainside, a counterpoint to the sniper's own discharge.

St. Pierre's body jerked once, flipping sideways as the bullet found its mark. A spray of crimson mingled with the snowflakes in the air. His ruined face stared out over the slope, a giant felled not by a stone but by a bullet from the gun of a small woman.

She approached cautiously, weapon still aimed, concerned he might be playing her. His chest lay still. No puff of breath issued from his mouth. His eyes, which in life looked dead as a shark's, in death showed human feeling, glazed with surprise.

Snowflakes began to settle on his lifeless form, as if nature itself sought to reclaim him.

"He's down!" she yelled into the radio. "Are you safe?"

Her breaths came hard and fast. Why didn't Brenner answer? She kept her gun trained on the now motionless figure of St. Pierre, even as the truth settled in her heart like winter frost.

"Is he...?" Brenner's voice crackled through the radio, tentative.

"Down," she confirmed, her voice hollow. "Brenner, are you hit?"

"Negative." There was relief there, but also something else. Worry? Disbelief?

Ella's gaze did not waver from the fallen man before her. He'd been a hunter, playing games with human prey, but in the end, he was the one caught in the crosshairs. Ella felt no triumph, only the weighty acknowledgment of necessity.

It was over. She had ended it.

Chapter 23

Brenner stood at her side, the two of them shivering in the cold as lights flashed overhead and emergency vehicles meandered up the slaloming paths that led from the city to the wilderness.

Already, they'd both given two statements. And now, the two of them sat in the back of the SUV, shivering, cold, and waiting for permission to go home.

Neither of them moved.

Ella wasn't sure what to say. She'd known what she'd done. A good shot. That's what everyone was telling her.

She'd had no choice...

But a part of her knew the truth.

Even if she'd had a choice, she would've made the same one.

She shivered as the realization dawned.

She grimaced at the thought.

"You okay?" Brenner bent his dark head towards hers.

She nodded, then leaned against him, closing her eyes.

"Thanks," he whispered.

"Mhmm."

"I... I've been thinking," he said.

"Uh-oh," she smiled.

The two of them watched as a snowplow came through pushing aside drifts to make room for the coroner's vehicle. It was a morbid scene, but beautiful too in the Alaskan wilderness, facing the tableau of white.

"I... I don't think I'll ever care for anyone else like I do for you."

"Thanks," she said softly.

What else should a girl say?

He shifted, nervous, until his blue eyes looked directly into hers. "I... I want to ask you something."

She hesitated now, her cheeks reddening, not just from the cold. "What sort of something?"

"I mean... I know it's probably not the best timing," he muttered. "Just..."

She turned to him now, worried. Was he breaking up with her?

But no. Despite his bad leg, Brenner had hunkered down on the snow drift. It must have been an uncomfortable position for him. In one hand, he had a small piece of plastic. The sort of twist-tie one found on a loaf of bread. He'd formed it into a circle. "It's... not much. Yet. But I'll get a real one soon."

She stared at the makeshift ring.

"I... I've loved you since we were kids," he said simply. "You've saved my life."

"And you've saved mine."

"More than once," he finished. "I owe you more than my life, though." He smiled. "I smiled again."

She just watched him, hesitant, careful.

He twirled the small ring in his hand. Snorted in laughter as he glanced out at the coroner's van sloshing by. "How romantic, right?"

Ella just leaned over and kissed him on the cheek.

"So," he said awkwardly.

"So what?"

"Will you?"

"Will I what?" she said coyly, her heart strangely calm. As if she'd been expecting this. As if her soul had been waiting for this very moment.

He let out a slow breath, eyes searching her face. "You know what..."

She paused, smiled directly into his beautiful stormy eyes, then kissed him again.

The End.

Other Books by Georgia Wagner

The skeletons in her closet are twitching...

Genius chess master and FBI consultant Artemis Blythe swore she'd never return to the misty Cascade Mountains.

Her father—a notorious serial killer, responsible for the deaths of seven women—is now imprisoned, in no small part due to a clue she provided nearly fifteen years ago.

And now her father wants his vengeance.

A new serial killer is hunting the wealthy and the elite in the town of Pinelake. Artemis' father claims he knows the identity of the killer, but he'll only tell daughter dearest. Against her will, she finds herself forced back to her old stomping grounds.

Once known as a child chess prodigy, now the locals only think of her as 'The Ghostkiller's' daughter.

In the face of a shamed family name and a brother involved with the Seattle mob, Artemis endeavors to use her tactical genius to solve the baffling case.

Hunting a murderer who strikes without a trace, if she fails, the next skeleton in her closet will be her own.

Other Books by Georgia Wagner

A cold knife, a brutal laugh. Then the odds-defying escape.

Once a hypnotist with her own TV show, now, Sophie Quinn works as a full-time consultant for the FBI. Everything changed six years ago. She can still remember that horrible night. Slated to be the River Killer's tenth victim, she managed to slip her bindings and barely escape where so many others failed. Her sister wasn't so lucky.

And now the killer is back.

Two PHDs later, she's now a rising star at the FBI. Her photographic memory helps solve crimes, but also helps her to never forget. She saw the River Killer's tattoo. She knows what he sounds like. And now, ten years later, he's active again.

Sophie Quinn heads back home to the swamps of Louisiana, along the Mississippi River, intent on evening the score and finding the man who killed her sister. It's been six years since she's been home, though. Broken relationships and shattered dreams exist among the bayous, the rivers, the waterways and swamps of Louisiana; can Sophie find her way home again? Or will she be the River Killer's next victim to float downstream?

Free Books and More

Want to see what else the Greenfield authors have written? Go to the website.

Home - Greenfield Press

Or sign up to our newsletter where you will get sneak peeks, exclusive giveaways, behind the scenes content, and more. Plus, you'll be notified of Fan Pricing events when they occur and get exclusive offers from other authors.

Click the link or copy it carefully into your web browser.

Newsletter - Greenfield Press

Prefer social media? Join our thriving Facebook community.

Want to join the inner circle where you can keep up to date with everything? This is a free page on Facebook where you can hang out with likeminded individuals and enjoy discussing my books. There is cake too (but only if you bring it).

Facebook

About the Author

Georgia Wagner worked as a ghost writer for many, many years before finally taking the plunge into self-publishing. Location and character are two big factors for Georgia, and getting those right allows the story to flow seamlessly onto the page. And flow it does, because Georgia is so prolific a new term is required to describe the rate at which nerve-tingling stories find their way into print.

When not found attached to a laptop, Georgia likes spending time in local arboretums, among the trees and ponds. An avid cultivator of orchids, begonias, and all things floral, Georgia also has a strong penchant for art, paintings, and sculptures.

Printed in Great Britain
by Amazon